DID YOU WHI

by

KATE RIGBY

Copyright 2019 Kate Rigby

Cover Design adapted from Royalty Free Image at
www.shuttersock.com

Awarded Southern Arts Bursary 1991 as
'Where A Shadow Played'

All characters are fictional, and any resemblance to
anyone living or dead is accidental

Acknowledgements

To all those family and friends who've been a support to me, a heartfelt thanks.

For all those who struggle or who have ever struggled with their mental health

ONE

Bit by bit, Amanda is piecing Jo together.

Jo was the baby they threw in the dustbin nearly twenty-two years ago. What a black, smelly, start to life, in that cylindrical tin coffin. Yes, it was a start and not a finish to life, because Jo is still alive today. Somewhere.

Jo's guardians must have found her wrapped in an old Daily Telegraph under old tea leaves and rotting potato peelings. They will have wiped her free of tea stains and thought, Finders Keepers. They'll have tried to make her their own but they'll never have made her whole because Jo still bleeds from having her other half ripped off. She will share the pain of parting. She will know what it is to have grown up without her reflection.

Jo is the twin sister Amanda has never seen, except in her mind's eye. It's in spiritual terms that Jo is most clearly defined. Jo's spirit is pearly-pink or green or blue. Iridescent. Amanda thinks every person has a psychic colour, although she's not sure she has one of her own.

She can't remember when she first became aware of that naked feeling all around her, that wind-chill sometimes to her left, sometimes to her right, but always spelling out the same lonely message: something is missing. Some*one* is missing. Jo. She no longer knows where the coast ends and where the sea begins with herself and Jo.

Jo is her twin sister she has never seen. But she has seen her stepsister most days, for nearly ten years. She and Angie have been growing towards each other over time and today they're not so unalike, though they have different surnames because her own mother, Rosalind, and stepfather, Neville, have never married. This means that she and Angie aren't legally stepsisters, but it's easier to think of themselves as such. Neville's soul is sort of brownish in colour, but a nice unimposing brown, a bit like the man.

Neville's soul is sort of brownish in colour, but a nice unimposing brown, a bit like the man.

Neville is an antique dealer. Rodney, the twins' real father was a lawyer when he was alive with an apt surname – Court – also her birthright. Rodney Court interests her a great deal because her mother rarely discusses him. She dismisses him in an instant. "It's so long ago now, Amanda, I simply can't remember." Or, "The past is dead and buried. What's the point of raking it up?" Consequently Rodney has developed rather a green spirit - the colour of mystery and summer ponds. Or perhaps unripeness or verdigris. Her mother's redness naturally complements Rodney's green. Red is a colour that attracts and after Rodney died, her mother had another lover before settling for Neville. But for every male admirer, her mother has lost the equivalent in female friendship. She has never been your Coffee Morning or Tupperware Party person and as she isn't working she has few new routes to company.

But at least her mother is complete which is more than can be said for her estranged twins. Amanda knows she can no longer wait for Jo to come home. She must go out and look for her, and soon. Very soon. Otherwise Jo might die in ignorance.

*

Billy Latham has only been going out with Angie Slattery for a matter of weeks although he knew her at school.

He likes her a lot. He sees her as a fun-loving creature with serious undertones; more creative than clever-clever.

He doesn't like girls who are clever clogses. Angie writes poetry, or so she says, though he hasn't been allowed to see any of it yet, but it seems to fit with that scatty way she has, like leaving umbrellas on buses or walking round town with her hem looped up – all part of her charm. Maybe neurotic would be a better choice of word - she certainly suffers from nervous heads and tight stomachs, a bit too frequently for his liking.

He recalls the occasion he first noticed Angie. He was a sixth former dating a fifth form girl called Maggie Rice whose face he can barely recall now. One afternoon in the parent-free Rice household, two of Maggie's friends were dancing in brilliant sunshine on the rickety old balcony there. They were doing a ghastly rendition of 'Strawberry Fields' and proceeded to work their way through a host of other Beatles' songs, each one sounding more dreadful than the last. One of the girls had a banana as her microphone, the other a peppermill. That was Angie, with the peppermill. They were clearly having a ball and that appealed. He's always liked a girl who knows how to enjoy herself.

The balcony cabaret was several years ago. He and Angie met again last summer, quite by chance. Even through his sunglasses, and several years of elapsed time he knew it was her. They were (and still are) both working in central Liverpool, he in the bank and she in the haberdashery section at the department store. They went for a few lunch-time drinks, reminisced about the good old teenage years, but it was to be October before they went on their first proper date. They went to Kirklands wine bar and on the way home kissed under the streetlamp on the corner of her road.

He lives in Waterloo, Liverpool 22, she in the more select area of Blundellsands, Liverpool 23. It takes him about ten minutes to walk from his door to hers. He likes the walk and the way the houses change in style and grandeur as he moves nearer to Angie's. He also likes the sound of the trains approaching along the main Liverpool to Southport line that, at a distance, sound like the galloping of mechanical hooves.

Angie's house has bay windows, three storeys and a name: Atherton House. He's always thought it classy, a house with a name. Atherton House is a magnificent product of Victorian workmanship; vertical, dark and serious like the people of its day. Angie lives here with her stepsister, father, stepmother and the family cat, Tinker. Atherton House isn't what you would call welcoming. Neither is Amanda when she answers the door. If he described her as vertical and serious, that would be too generous – she is appallingly neutral. They have met a few times but much of it is unmemorable. Her voice is small, almost an apology for a voice, unlike Angie who gives life to her words. In fact, Amanda is a bit of an apology for a person, she is just there - quiet and tractable as a servant. Every time he meets her he has a job remembering her line of work. He knows it's in some office but he can't remember any more than that, though she must have told him two or three times at least. But after being told so many times he dare not ask again.

"Angie's got a migraine," Amanda says as he steps into the hall. It's a dark hall with antique furniture.

"Not again," he says. "She had two last week. She knows I've got tickets for tonight."

"For *Cabaret,* wasn't it?"

"Yeah, a mate of mine has got a small part – and I've also booked a table at our favourite restaurant beforehand, so she's got to come."

"She can't do anything when she gets a migraine."

"Ah, she can't let me down now – she's known about this for ages."

Rosalind appears from the lounge, cat at her heels. He likes Rosalind. She is both welcoming and confident.

"Hi Billy," she says, offering him a cigarette.

"I've given up, Rosalind."

"The fags or Angie?"

He smiles. "You may well ask. I hope she's not trying to give me the Big E or nothing."

"Of course not. I'd come with you myself, Billy, only I'm going out myself tonight."

"I've wearing my best kecks an' all."

"You could always take Amanda," suggests Rosalind. "She's not doing anything this evening."

*

Billy wonders what on earth he has let himself in for as he waits with Amanda on Blundellsands station for the train into town. As he stands in silence on the platform, a good yard apart from the gauche Amanda, he wishes he hadn't sold his car. At least they would be half way to Liverpool by now. It seems an eternity before he hears that twang on the lines below, signalling an approaching train.

Billy observes his fellow travellers, in an effort to pass the time: the men hiding behind their newspapers on their way home from work – no faces, no communication; the lads, like that one there, furtively reading that girl's book over her shoulder; those cheeky schoolboys, plotting mischief.

It's not only the character of the people making the journey exciting. It's the character of the city, thickening as you near its heart – suburbs giving way to dockland. He points out his favourite landmarks on the way, laying a hand as he does so on Amanda's wooden arm, forgetting.

They alight at Liverpool Central and he feels a sense of unease as they walk through town to the restaurant,

9

almost ashamed to be out with such a dead-leg. When they arrive, the waiter takes Amanda's thick winter coat and shows them to their romantic table for two. The waiter lights the bottled candle between them and hands them each a menu.

Billy looks across at Amanda. "What d'you fancy?"
"What are you having?"
"Kebab and rice."
"I'll have the same as you."

After the waiter has taken their orders and brought over their bottle of Mateus Rose – Angie's favourite – a thick silence descends. He can't help noticing the sensible navy blue dress Amanda is wearing – not like the black sexy number you can expect from Angie. And her hair is long and straight and dark brown – not Angie's dark, wavy and exuberant plume. But he is stuck with Amanda for the evening so he may as well make the most of it.

"Do you know *Cabaret* at all?"
"I don't think so."
"You've never seen it on the telly, you know, with Liza Minnelli? You must have heard the songs. *Come to the cabaret old chum, life is a cabaret.* No?"

She smiles at least. Yes, he's noticed this about her – she smiles quite readily but it's indiscriminate.

"D'you like plays?"
"I don't mind."
"D'you ever go and see any?"
She gives a nervous laugh. "Not many."
"So what do you like to do?"
"I don't know really." She twiddles the stem of her glass.
"How do you fill your spare time?"
She shrugs. "The usual, you know. TV, music."
"What about footie?"
"Not really."

"Tennis or athletics?"

"I don't like sport much."

"God, did anyone ever tell you you're hard work?"

She smiles again. Infuriating. Every avenue of conversation seems to arrive at the same dead-end. What on earth made her tick?

When the kebabs arrive they eat in silence. He finds himself sinking into introspection over Angie's migraines. Were they real? What if they turn out to be serious? What if she has another fella? What if, what if, what if.

"Does Angie know what causes these migraines of hers?"

"Stress she thinks."

"Oh what, the prospect of going out for a meal and the theatre afterwards? Very stressful!"

The silence returns, and he resumes his thoughts of Angie. So what if she has a migraine? It's no big deal. Doesn't her appeal lie in her complex and unpredictable nature? But he realizes he is not so much baffled by Angie's ailments as irritated at having a potentially interesting evening spoiled, and the sight of the ungainly girl across the table does little to alleviate matters. She could at least feel some sisterly obligation and try to compensate. Fat chance! She never shows any bold initiative. She never says or does anything to please or offend, she is incapable of making a simple decision unless someone else has endorsed it first, even down to her choice of food it would seem. Still waters run deep, they say, but her neutrality is a symptom of shallowness surely. He's rarely seen her engrossed in a book or newspaper, which would account for her threadbare conversation and formless opinions. She has nothing to declare.

He decides he can't bear to sit through another painful course and is grateful when Amanda follows his example and declines dessert.

He is greatly relieved to get to *Cabaret*. Here he loses himself in the thrill of the music and colour and dance, and forgets Amanda is even there.

*

On a raw Saturday, late January, Angie looks up to an ice-rink sky. Winter birds fly across it, like pieces of charred newspaper from a bonfire. She tracks the telegraph wires, allowing herself to gaze skywards as she did as a child. She regrets that adult heads miss so much up there, moored as they are to matters on the ground: work and saving for this and that and rushing hither and thither. As far as she's concerned there's really only one person who's a footstool back to the heavens and that's Amanda. She can't really say the same about Billy though she supposes she might be Billy's footstool.

Today is her twenty-fourth birthday. People all around her are breathing wintry wreaths on the air. Perhaps one or two of them even share her birthday. You are blessed on your birthday. You can do what you want. When she gets home she will ask Amanda a big favour – one Amanda won't be able to refuse her on her birthday.

Once home, she goes up to her yellow bedroom on the top floor, the one across the landing from Amanda's pale green one, and lays out the black dress she has just bought on her bed where Amanda is sitting, waiting for her opinion to be sought.

Angie tries on the dress and gives a quick twirl. "Well? What do you think?"

"It's nice."

Amanda is so sweet. She would never say if she thought it ghastly.

"What about at the back? Does it look OK?"

"Fine. Are you wearing it tonight?"

"I think so. Billy says he likes me in black," she says,

grabbing hold of her matching clutch bag, to complete the desired effect. She then undoes the zip and steps out of the dress. "I love birthdays. All the fuss and the cards and the cake and everyone being nice, don't you?"

"No, I loathe it. I can't wait for it to be over."

"Oh you always say that but you don't mean it." But she knows Amanda does. She knows Amanda despises the individual focus that birthdays bring, unlike Christmas, which is a celebration for all.

"Amanda? I want to ask you a favour."

"You want to borrow those earrings Neville gave me for Christmas."

"No, nothing like that. Something different."

"What's that?"

"Well, I know this sounds mad…" Angie reaches for her lip salve and moistens each lip with it, buying herself a few crucial seconds of composure. "But I'd like to borrow some of your poems."

"My poems? Why?"

"Please don't say no, Amanda." Angie rubs her newly-salved lips together. "Not on my birthday."

"I'm not. I just don't know what you can want with them. They're rubbish."

"No they're not. Look, I don't know how to say this – it's just that I told Billy some time back that I wrote poetry. I don't know why I said it but I probably thought it would impress him at the time."

"And now he's asked to see some."

"Put it this way, Amanda. He's expressed an interest. I've put him off so far but he just thinks I'm being modest. I wondered if you'd mind helping me out – if I get pushed into a corner."

"That's OK. I don't mind."

"Oh Amanda, you're an angel!" She reaches down and hugs her. "He just won't drop the subject. It probably won't be necessary though – with any luck he'll forget about it."

*

Several weeks later, Amanda sits behind the French window in the living room writing a poem. The mood only takes her now and then. She looks up and lets her eyes rove the garden where a robin has just landed on the rooted spade. Other birds too are hopping and stopping on the grey March grass. An inclement wind is now drying out the rain that, twenty minutes earlier, it had hurled in bucketfuls against the glass panes. Everything is late this year: there are still only snowdrops, not a crocus in sight, let alone daffodils.

The house is empty but it's never quiet during these moments. It's like listening to air in a seashell. There's often an undefined sound behind the emptiness which she can't quite put her finger on. She gets up from her unshaped poem on the living room table and looks up at the servants' panel above the door. In the old days, if a bell sounded in the house, the servants would have looked to this panel to discover which room had rung: the dining room, bedroom one, bedroom two, and so on. Even today, the ring of a bell is accompanied by a vibrating marker in the bell panel, indicating the room concerned. Now, though there's no outward sound, there's a slight reverberation, an almost imperceptible shiver of movement from the little window in the panel, marked bedroom two.

This is the spare bedroom on the first floor, opposite her mother's and Neville's room, where bits of old junk are stored, and where the rowing machine lives – its novelty having worn off for Neville and Rosalind, though they used to exercise on it twice daily. Tinker, the cat, also sleeps in this room. Amanda creeps up there and pushes the door open. She seems to know what she is looking for. She finds it peeping out from under the cat-litter tray – the fate of many an old newspaper. It's quite faded now and four months old, but there's something in here calling her attention.

Then she finds it. It's an article about people who have been trying to trace a lost family member and there, embedded in the heart of the piece, is Jo's story. (Well, here Jo is actually referred to as Joanna. Funny, she always thought her Jo was a Josephine, but it just goes to show how mistaken you can be sometimes.) Joanna is appealing to find her real family. She is aged twenty-one at the time of writing, born and bred in Liverpool, now living in Devon. Her adoptive parents, now dead, knew little of Jo's family of origin. Apart from this, there is little more to go on, except for poor-quality photos of the appellants, some of them in virtual silhouette.

Amanda waits for the feeling of shock to pass, and when it does she can hardly contain herself. It has taken her quest a giant leap forward. Some clues at last. This is what genealogical discoveries must be like, when, after pursuing a cold trail for months or years, you suddenly hit on that missing link. She knows she has to go to Devon. She has none of her usual second thoughts or trouble making up her mind. It's suddenly all very clear. What is there for her here apart from a dead-end job in an antiquated office in Bootle?

She will miss Angie lots, of course, but Angie isn't her true sister. Jo is. And Jo must take priority.

*

It surprises Rosalind a little that Amanda is telephoning around for hotel jobs in Devon. She sees Amanda is quite determined. She's always taken Amanda to be a sticker, not someone who acts on a whim or impulse – that is more Angie's style of doing things. But then perhaps Angie has unconsciously influenced her, shaken her out of her routine.

People often say to Rosalind – on learning that it is in fact Amanda who is her blood relative and not Angie – "Oh really? I thought it was the other way round. Angie is a lot like you." And it makes Rosalind feel quite guilty if she enjoys the compliment, which she invariably does, because Angie is very attractive, Amanda more plain. From a physical perspective, it is fairly obvious why people make this assumption: Angie has the same thick, dark hair as herself and animated mannerisms.

Rosalind, however, sees herself as a lot stronger than Angie. For instance, Angie seems to have some minor ailment every other day. Neville has suggested Angie go back to the doctor but Angie seems to share Rosalind's own horror of anything medical. Another overlap between herself and her stepdaughter…

"I've got myself a couple of interviews," Amanda announces suddenly, pulling Rosalind up short. "In Paignton."

TWO

During her first fortnight at her new job in Paignton – a time period protracted and packed with impressions - Amanda makes a pledge to be the Angie of Devon. Each day, her chambermaid duties completed at the three star Heathfield Hotel, she takes a stroll along the shore. She refuses to waste the sun. That fresh woody scent of April stirs things inside her, something dry summer heat can never do.

Today she follows her usual route and heads for the sea front. As she crosses the road she thinks, *though it's only ten steps from kerb to kerb there's the road in between.* She doesn't know why this thought should come into her head or what it means. She walks with the purposeless pace of the old, but her head is thrown back Angie-style, proud and bright as a sunflower. She finds the harbour pretty with its boats – red, blue, yellow – jingling and bobbing on a shrinking sheet of water that will soon become a sloppy floor of mud.

The seasonal workers are unlocking everything for the first time since last year, in preparation for Easter. Out come the postcards, the beach balls, the luminous windmills, the seafood delicacies, the sticks of rock. Amanda walks around the harbour onto the sand-dusted promenade, plunging her hands deep into her pockets. The fresh salty air unwinds spools of hope, like invisible streamers behind her. She smiles to herself. She is happy walking alone. Happy and self-contained.

The sea is medicine. It's anonymous like she is. She likes the feeling of being unknown, it gives her power and lots of room for manoeuvre. She drops herself into the cobbled sand and looks along the coastline in the direction of Torquay. She imagines there might be small recesses and tucks along the way: dark moody coves with huge clammy boulders and cold mossy seaweed where in summer flocks of children will fish for crabs and starfish.

Directly ahead, the tide is on the turn again. The odd dog sniffs at the strewn array of planks, bottles, ropes, dropped off by the last tide. She watches as the sands are devoured minute by minute by the waves, fanning and fizzing into a foamy braid. Some of the waves have a ragged hemline and the foam seems to float around like jaded dishwater...

A small immortal child appears on the empty shore. She jets from the waves or did she crystallize from the clouds? The child plays, laughs, blossoming from dust. There's always a home for the child-Jo Amanda never knew. Jo loves the sea air. It's as if she can't breathe enough of it; as if she still tastes dustbin. Jo should have company and here they come: the children in their jumble-sale clothes. Like iron filings or the children of Hamelin they have been drawn out of their city Lego-blocks. Today they wear white robes and garlands of flowers about their heads. They are greeted and baptized by the Sacred Mermaid, the Anointed One, the Queen of the Sea. Tomorrow they will return to their cities with regenerated spirit. The ghetto will never again reflect in their eyes. Their eyes will be organs reincarnated. These children are young, pretty, aspiring – one of the girls was once a carnival princess and her brother played Joseph in a nativity play. They have the determination and spark of Anne Frank.

But they grow, don't they? A new generation saunters unceremoniously through the sand, scuffing it with their mighty clodhoppers, scratching inane messages in its fudgy surface. Tina luvs Darren. KL woz ere. Man United. They giggle. They are all of them awkward, self-conscious, vacuous. At the same time, showy. Big show-offs. They have jettisoned their early ambitions in favour of the peer group. Mutinous, stroppy nobodies, spitting and swearing. Something shocking has ravaged their purity, after all, like blood on snow. Adolescence.

But it's just another stage, like all the others, and, like the defaced sand, it too will be washed away with no trace. Their giggles will become sedate smiles, their awkwardness replaced by a sort of tame confidence. Uniformity and adolescence will make their exit together – hand in hand – and in their place individuality will begin to bloom.

*

Amanda sits in a café near the sea front. By the time she gets to the unstirred sugary mud at the bottom of her second cup, the sun has nearly drowned in the chilly sea.

She leaves the café and drifts away along the prom. The white horses on the sea are pink with evening and she can see the lights of neighbouring towns twinkling in the distance. Jo may be sitting at one of those windows, waiting, nursing the pain of her wound. *It's OK, Jo. I am near.*

It's almost time for her protective kingfisher to clock off and make way for the night shift worker, her screech owl – always her pillar of fire by night.

*

The only part of the hotel occupied at the moment is the wing they call the Hacienda: a brand new annexe which still has that delicious smell of taps hardly turned, wood not yet shiny, paint not yet faded. They must have worked round the clock in the winter to have it all ready for the new season.

Amanda delights in the fact that there's only one other

chambermaid sharing the work with her: an older lady called Maude who is non-resident. A quiet, innocuous sort of person. They will be taking on more staff in June, it is said, but as yet the other hotel workers are unimposing, no sticky-burr types.

During their very first mornings – each one piquant with a chill April gold – she and Maude put on their stripy brown and white overalls and reported to the housekeeper for their duties. They were given spring-cleaning jobs to do, like cleaning the walls and windows and fire doors. Even sweeping up dead woodlice.

Now things have got busier and each morning she and Maude are given a list of occupied rooms to do. If they're lucky all the rooms will be stays – except on Saturdays, of course, the big changeover day, when they will nearly all be departures and even those staying on for two weeks will require clean sheets. Sometimes there are departures during the week as well. Departures are good, on the one hand, since you might be left a tip in the ashtray or under a cup and saucer on the tea tray. You can also move around the rooms with ease, free as they are of holiday clutter. On the other hand, departures require a lot more work and are back-breaking. She has, however, managed to get her departures down to a fine art, now only taking about half an hour per room.

Once she has her list, she collects her yellow bucket and replenishes any empty stocks from the store cupboard. In her bucket she carries cleaners, polish, a duster, a cloth, sacks, bin-liners, teas, coffees, milks, sugars. And soaps. The little white soaps have Heathfield Hotel engraved on their fondant surfaces and look good enough to eat. They're packed tightly together like biscuits or special confectionary leaving little flaked-off bits at the bottom of the box. That done, her final task is to collect a hoover, one in good working order, before making her way over to her particular patch of the Hacienda: Rooms 1 to 12.

Today, as on other days, she begins with Room 12. She always works backwards because Rooms 11 and 12 take the longest to do. They are, in fact, special rooms. Room 12 is a bridal suite with gold taps in the bathroom. She feels very privileged to have these rooms on her list. Today, however, there's a DO NOT DISTURB sign on the door. Room 11 is empty – the door to an unoccupied room is usually propped open – and so she moves on to Room 10, knocks on the door and takes the master key from her overall pocket in readiness to enter.

The first thing she always does is to switch the radio on. The bedside radios only receive Radios 2, 3 and 4. She usually ends up listening to Radio 2 – a good background sort of station. She hooks her duster into her belt and brushes sand out of the double bed with her hand. She then straightens out the bottom sheet and has to re-do the hospital corners, but by now the routine is so automatic it frees her to think of other things. In the en suite bathroom she considers how lucky she is to have a job where she is largely left alone to think. She's very thankful to be a chambermaid behind the scenes than, say, a waitress, who is very much at the forefront of things, a little like being on stage. She folds the bath towels and remembers why she came here. For Jo. Though now she is in Devon, much of the urgency has faded. She can relax in the knowledge of Jo's nearness. If she is totally honest, she has been completely sidetracked from her mission by this new job. But it will soon be time to continue the search, now that she has settled into her new surroundings. Where should she start though? Devon is a big county and she doesn't even have Jo's surname. Why wasn't Jo's surname included in the article? It wasn't as if she wanted to remain anonymous or anything like that. Perhaps she was trying to protect her adoptive parents, but they were dead, didn't the article say? Perhaps interested readers were meant to write to the address that (probably) appeared at the end of the article. But she'd been so bowled over by that new lead, she had overlooked such practical details, or maybe the contact details had been torn by time and cat paw marks.

When she has finished with Room 10, she nips over to the staff chalets. When she first heard she was to be living in a chalet she pictured something Swiss and timbered, half-way up a cliff, but of course there is little resemblance. The chalets are pokey and basic, almost like glorified sheds, though some have sea views. She has a partial view of the sea, but it's obscured by the tradesman's entrance to the hotel with its great metal fire escape and cylindrical, institutional bins.

At least Jo wasn't disposed of in one of these bins, where she might have contracted salmonella. Where she may have been lost forever in some landfill site. You have to be grateful for At Leasts.

*

In June the sticky burr people arrive.

They attach their hooks to kitchens, bedrooms, the restaurant, the still room. No place is sacred any longer. Along the corridors there are now strange chambermaids setting impossible standards. She hears one of them say, and not even as a brag, that it takes her fifteen minutes to do a Departure. Fifteen minutes! Who can compete with that? But there's worse. Another pair of girls, Linda and Val, have taken over the Hacienda, resulting in the premature resignation of the innocuous Maude. Amanda has been moved to the old wing, and within days is joined by a brash London girl called Dee. Dee, with her head of tight red curls and toothy grin, wastes no time in advertizing her presence. She somehow always manages to pick the noisiest hoover – quite apt really – and on her first day is already swooping on Amanda.

"Cor, what a palaver," she says. "I'm going for a fag break. Coming?"

"I don't smoke."

"No kiddin'. Two months more of this and you'll be smokin', drinkin', the whole hog. Come and keep me company anyway."

Amanda follows, somewhat reluctantly, because her first impressions of Dee don't augur well. But past experience has shown her that first impressions can be misleading; that you can end up loving those who you initially hated and vice versa. But more immediate than this is the fearful prospect of a friendship with this girl. It comes as a relief, therefore, to see Dee chatting up waiters or sounding out the other girls about the local night life.

By her second or third day, Dee is completely at home, something which astounds Amanda who has never felt at home anywhere.

"You know that waitress, Marjie, with the dark curly hair? She's going to fix us up with butters and marmalades and we're gonna sort out teas and coffees and milks for her."

After another few days, Dee has written off most of her fellow workers. "There aren't half some stuffy gits here," she says, slouching into Amanda's bed at the end of their shift. "I mean Steve's OK, he's a laugh, and the other girls doing the rooms but that's about it. I don't *fancy* anyone here. Do you?"

"I haven't really thought about it."

"It's the first thing I think about it." Dee slips off her shoes and blows smoke everywhere. "Did you say you'd done hotel work before?"

"No."

"You ain't got much to go on then, Mand. You seen that revolting porter Ray? I'm telling you there's one of them at every hotel. He stinks like a skunk an' all. No wonder he's so sex-starved. Never shuts up about it."

"I should suggest a shower and a therapist."

Dee cackles into the pillow and Amanda is pleased to have prompted such a response in Dee. Over the years she has acquired some of the 'right' things to say, after all, and occasionally finds she's quick enough to slot in such a quip at the right point.

"When's your day off then, Mand?"

"Tomorrow."

"Me too! We can paint the town tonight then. Lie in tomorrow. Down the beach in the afternoon if it's nice. What d'you reckon?"

"Yeah OK." Amanda feigns delight, though really she feels a wave of resentment. There will be no more days alone on the beach or listening to the ting-ting-ting of the boat masts in the harbour if she allows others to butt into her free time and demand her company. A counter-wave immediately washes the thought away. Friends are essential, aren't they? She is lucky – isn't she? – to have earned Dee's friendship, so quickly, with so little effort. In fact, earned seems hardly an appropriate word at all in the circumstances. She must learn to be more altruistic with her time.

*

At nine o'clock, a prinked-up Dee knocks on Amanda's chalet door, next door but one to her own. The purple dress clashes violently with the flame frizz but Dee can carry it off. Her neck is collared in a row of tawdry pearls and over her gold-freckled shoulder is the shiniest black handbag you ever saw.

So this is the beginning. The beginning of regular

nights out with Dee, three, maybe four times a week. The beginning of the end. On Fridays and Saturdays, the favourite venue is a club called The Rendezvous, a small sty of a place and what the more discerning club-goer would call a bit of a dive.

Before long, Amanda starts dressing up too in bright colours. She takes up smoking. This is what you do to keep in with your friends. You become as they are.

Dee's need for a generous measure of male company is satiated in the night clubs. When she is with boys, Dee moves, speaks, laughs, with a new kind of energy. Dee has two laughs, making her easy to spot in a crowd: the laugh which rattles harshly like a road-drill and the softer, more seductive one, like gurgly water. This is the one she turns on for the boys she fancies. If Amanda washes down enough Pils or Carlsberg Special, she too can lose herself in the loud music, the dancing, the men. At eleven o'clock, she is still in the running, a likely contestant in this competition, but by one o'clock, if not puking in the ladies', she normally suffers – in some dim alcove – some squid-eyed youth with steamy lips over her own; his clammy hands wriggling down her bra. Over her shoulder she will see others cordoned here in similar postures, enjoying or enduring, depending on their mood.

Sometimes Dee will head for the alcove too, and every once in a while actual conversations may break from sore, passion-worn lips. But not very often. Not intelligent ones anyway. Yet Amanda has noticed how easy it is to discuss things of a personal or intimate nature with these holidaying or seasonal men who she'll probably never see again: things she's never even discussed with Angie, and it is totally liberating. She's able to slip Jo into the conversation surreptitiously. Inconsequently. And it doesn't matter at all. No one cares that much.

Because no one is listening that much.

THREE

Amanda considers how she was like a sole trader when she first arrived in Paignton. This then evolved into a sort of partnership once she met Dee, and now they too have expanded like an ink-blot into a kind of limited company – the Linda-Val-Marjie one.

She has sipped them all, like you might as a newcomer to alcohol, and gone through hating each of them in turn. For instance, she loathed Linda at first, much preferring Val who seemed mild and potable like Shandy, but she has since amended her opinion and now thinks Linda is better than Val. Val is a petite, bloodless girl who goes in for the muttering of sarcastic innuendos and whose worst shortcoming seems to be her quietness. Amanda hates other quiet people: she likes people to be complementary to herself. Linda, on the other hand, is sophisticated and scented, like wine, but she can go to your head if you're not careful. Linda stares into heads, with those dreamy liquid eyes, like drops of unset chocolate.

While for Marjie there has been no second opinion. Amanda hated her from the start. Marjie can appear dreamy but it's a deceptive dreaminess – Marjie is completely on the ball. She has the kind of Liverpool accent that is arresting – sort of slow and clear and intelligent – and her laughter is catching like a yawn. She is adored for her ideas, suggestions, clothes. She has dark, risible eyes and a face that creases into fetching little folds and dimples when she smiles, and she doesn't walk so much as swagger. She is what men called well-endowed. She is a man's girl and this, together with her evening work, means that her time spent with the others is mercifully kept to a minimum. She is the bitter liqueur of the company – you either permit her to singe your throat or you clear your mouth of her heavy burning.

Tonight, Amanda and Linda wait while Dee clots her eyelashes with mascara before another of their nocturnal excursions. Linda irons her hands proudly down her black pencil-skirt and, with a tulip-straight back, picks up the magazine on the bed, folded back to the stars' forecast page. "What's your star sign?"

"Libra," says Dee. "Same as yours."

"Not yours face-ache. I was asking Amanda."

"Pisces."

"That's March, isn't it? Don't know much about those. How old were you last birthday then?"

"Twenty-two."

"Were you? I thought you were younger than me."

"Shit!" Dee sighs, lifting a moist pad to her eye and smearing away her eye-shadow. "I'm gonna have to start again on this eye."

"Did you say you'd got brothers and sisters, Amanda?"

She colours. Not gradually, but a full-blown blush exploding across her face. Linda is poised to engulf her reply, fish-like. At least Dee keeps off personal ground.

"A sister. Have you?" she says, quickly diverting the attention away from the empty space that is her. The space waiting to be filled by her secret sister.

But how perfectly the fish leaps for the bait. Linda is soon absorbed in her own family and Amanda keeps up a succession of questions until Linda looks at her watch. "Oh come on, Dee. It'll be ten o'clock at this rate by the time we get out."

"Val's not here yet, so you've got to wait anyway."

"No we haven't. Val's not feeling well."

"Oh now she tells me. What's up with her anyway? Too much to drink last night I expect."

"Something like that. She was on the Black Russians last night."

Linda catches Dee wiping away yet another fruitless eye design. "Bloody hell, Dee! We'll never get out. We'll go on our own in a minute if we have to."

"You bleedin' well do that then," Dee hisses, her eyes not flinching from her displeasing reflection.

"It's just that we're wasting valuable drinking time sitting here, not to mention all the blokes who'll have already clicked by the time we get down there – and all for the sake of your vanity!"

"Oh hark at her! I wouldn't be doing this if I was so bleedin' perfect now would I, daft bitch. It's only them what thinks they're so gorgeous that spends no time in front of the mirror, ain't it?"

Their arguing and swearing embarrasses Amanda, not through any offence it has caused her, not even because she is a bit of a pawn on their battleground, but because she is herself incapable of partaking in such a row. It confounds her that a pair of girls of such brief acquaintance can argue so freely. She has never quarrelled with anyone here, or they with her. Arguments are for family and friends; it is only acquaintances that are always agreeable and polite with one another.

She takes such care to fit in with their every move. She thinks how every personality has a thousand different sculptors working on it year in year out, fashioning, molding, and shaping, to make it what it is. She too can feel her own being carved and chiselled at every day by her friends, and the worst thing about it is that Marjie has

29

left her odious stamp. In Marjie's presence, Amanda feels her voice drifting into that self-assured sing-song. Here and there she catches herself swaggering along the corridor, smiling that sweet-and-sour smile.

She feels she is little more than a conglomeration of them all, though they don't seem to notice. They have no need to argue with her because it would be like arguing with themselves: she is just a mirror for their reflections. She doesn't know how to delete them from her self and decides it is simplest to keep up the pretence. Dee and the others are straightforward people, clear as glass. They live prosaic lives which lack romance – not their niggardly idea of romance, but real romance. The stuff of fiery poetry or mysticism or art. She has to rely on outside stimulation: conversational snippets in shops, along the street, on the next table in the cafe, on the radio. She doesn't want her brain to lie like a dead nest beneath the rafters of her skull.

And so the mutual politeness prevails with Dee and Co. But she feels excluded by their increasing familiarity, their cryptic laughter. It is unshareable and eclipsed in privacy, like other peoples' dreams.

*

One hot day in July, she sits with the chambermaids and one of the waiters on the terrace by the chalets. Marjie, fortunately, is otherwise engaged. Taff, the gormless young waiter with strawberry-blond hair and a face full of pimples, is larking around as usual. There is much good-sported bickering between the girls and the boy, every day sex play - though none of them remotely desires him. Dee has him in stitches and tells him rude jokes, whereas he admires Linda's confidence and sense of class as he calls it. And he finds Val's quiet sensitivity most engaging, (yes, even Val's shyness is seen as graceful), but the length of time his inane eyes pass

Amanda's way is negligible. She feels herself to be an awkward affix and is mortified that even someone as unappealing as Taff doesn't think she is worth a second look.

Dee scrapes her plastic bucket-chair along the paving. "Oy Taff. Coming for a swim then?"

"I haven't got me trunks on."

"Even better."

"I suppose I can roll my trousers up."

"Oh bor-*ring*."

Amanda, Linda and Val watch as Dee and Taff pick their way through sunbathers and skim the searing white sand like hot coals as they head towards the sea. Val turns her attention to comparing tans. "You brown as quick as toast, Linda," she says enviously, looking with disapproval at her own faint coating of sugar-pink on her arms and legs.

"Come on you three!" Dee shouts from the kerb of the sea. "Don't be chicken!"

"Huh, I'll show her who's chicken," says Linda, rising to her feet. "Aren't you two coming?"

"I'll stay here and watch our stuff," says Amanda, hoping Val will go down and join them so she can be alone.

"What about you, Val?"

"Period pains."

"Oh well, you can keep Amanda company."

So she is left with the dreadful Val. She hates to be stuck with one other person because she feels totally responsible for their entertainment; for making the conversation flow. In a group, on the other hand, you can get away with not speaking at all if you wish.

"I haven't had any period pains since doing this job," Amanda says, in an effort to clear the awkward silence. "That's one thing you can say for it."

"Well, I must say mine haven't been as bad as normal. I usually have to go to bed on the first day."

"How many rooms did you have to do this morning?"

"Twelve, I think."

"How many departures?"

"About four. I can't remember now."

"Four? That's quite a lot for a Tuesday, isn't it?"

"I suppose so." Val looks decidedly disinterested. "Anyway we've finished work for today so any more boring work-talk is banned from the conversation from now on, OK?"

Banned? This is the only area of conversation that feels safe; that flows. But there seems to be an unwritten rule that dictates what you can talk about and, more importantly, when. The rule says you can talk about work in work but not outside. It's the same when they go to the nightclubs. She likes to hide behind work-talk but the others frown upon it. Somehow you are considered stuffy or peculiar if you linger on work matters too long.

So what does she talk about next? There are diminishing possibilities the more you get to know someone. With strangers, the boys in the nightclubs for example, the sky is the limit. But with so-called friends, you can so easily exhaust your store.

*

At the end of July, Angie and Billy come down to visit Amanda for a week and stay at a nearby campsite. Every day of their visit the heat is intense and arid, like desert heat. "You don't get brown in this sort of heat," complains Angie. "You just sweat." The sands too have been totally covered by a fruity spread of people and the Heathfield is full to the brim, meaning more sweat and toil for the hotel team. Amanda finds it quite unbearable having to strip beds and hoover floors in solar-hot rooms, and she frequently has to sit down at the dressing-tables to wipe dried soap drips or other marks from mirrors with her towel. There she will sit for a few moments, sipping water, trying to recharge her strength, unable to think of anything much beyond what is in front of her, such as the box of pink tissues on each dressing table, one of the nice touches the Heathfield provides.

It's very comforting, therefore, at the end of each stint, to be greeted by home comforts in the form of Angie and Billy. The pair of them seem quite content to spend most of their days on the beach, sandwiched between air-beds and funny-shaped people massaging sun oil into each other's bodies and Punch and Judy, and beach missionaries with their red shirts and quasi-religious songs. Billy seems to find it fascinating to watch the British on holiday. "Look at that pair of divvies," he will say, wearing that T-shirt of his with the words *Wuckin Furries* printed in red over his chest. Angie, meanwhile, tries a new flavour of ice-cream every day before it melts down the side of her cone. "Oh I love these crisp Italian cones," she says each day. "They're so much better than those horrid orange cardboardy things."

Then one evening, towards the end of Angie and Billy's stay, Dee knocks on the door of Amanda's chalet.

"Sorry to bother you, Mand, but I've just heard about Marjie. Don't suppose you've heard nothing, have you?"

"Heard what?"

"She's leaving. Says she's got another job back home."

Amanda tries to conceal her delight. "Oh dear."

"Awful, ain't it? It all sounds pretty dodgy to me. She's not the kind of person who'd tell you, being proud and that but - promise you won't say nothing– "

"Promise." She can always keep a secret. She's kept the secret of Jo all her life.

"I reckon she got the push."

"She hasn't, has she? For what?"

"Oh they'll find any excuse," says Dee. "Clamping down, I suppose. Well, she wouldn't be the first, would she? What about those two bar staff they sacked last week? I'll be next if I'm not careful – all those sheets and towels I keep lifting." She drops her cigarette to the ground and stamps it out. "That your sister with you?"

"Yes. D'you want to come in?"

"I won't right now, Mand. Just on my way down the club. But say hi to them from me. I'll catch up with you later."

"Yeah, see you, Dee."

"Well I dunno," says Billy, as she comes in and pushes the door to. "We've been here nearly a week and we've hardly met any of your mates. So far we've met some decrepit porter for all of five minutes and had a brief chinwag with some waitress. I wouldn't mind but I love meeting new people."

"I'm sorry."

"Anyone'd think you're ashamed of us the way you've kept us apart."

"It's not that," she says. "Other staff have had their friends and families visit who I've hardly seen. They go off out for the day and do their own thing."

"OK, you're forgiven."

When it's time for Angie and Billy to leave, Amanda, like an unhappy child in care, wants to go with them. Dee and co haven't been missed at all. She's amazed, in fact, that she has persisted this long with this farcical slave-job. This isn't enjoyment – this is sufferance, and the thought of wrestling to be Dee's social equal for a moment longer, completely drains her.

*

By August, there are some shake-ups in the housekeeping department. The old housekeeper is sacked for being drunk once too often on duty and is replaced by an enormous, ambitious Welsh woman who is highly dissatisfied with the standard of the rooms.

"The open end of the pillow must face away from the door," she tells her chambermaids in her office one morning. "Didn't you know that? Now tuck the plug into the sink overflow, will you, girls? It looks so much tidier than a bloody dangling one." She looks at some notes scribbled on her pad. "Dee, your taps are awful. Valerie your baths are disgusting. I know some of the guests leave them in a bloody state but that's no excuse for you to do the same. I wouldn't leave my bath a mess. I always hear my mother's voice. She always said, 'Wash the bath after you, Glynis – the next person doesn't want to see your pubic hairs'. Watch you hear her words too. Amanda, you're taking too long over your rooms and your edges need doing."

The change of housekeeper, the volume of guests and the departure of Marjie seems to change the tone of the Heathfield. Everyone is burying themselves in their work; they are too busy for jokes, they are more tired, they are flagging a bit; that early season freshness has been lost - and of course Marjie is missed by most. But Amanda loves it. She loves this getting down to work attitude, this not having to do the rounds of nightclubs, this quieter life, and by the time things have crept back to before – regular nights out again, larking about at work – it is too late. She has already passed the point of no return. She has rediscovered her old friend solitude and has to invent more and more elaborate ruses to maintain that inner sanctum. Stomach aches, ignoring her door, letter-writing. But the girls are slow at taking a hint – it seems incomprehensible to them that anyone should wish to avoid them and so into her room they still troop, peering over her shoulder at her private work. No sooner has she picked up her pen than there it goes again – bang bang

bang. There is only one thing for it. To disappear off on her own where she can discover new walks, search for magic coves, and think. Where she can remember why she came. Her head now hangs like a waning flower, her eyes still searching the shore for clues; still waiting for the answer to be washed up on the tide like buried treasure.

Then one night she has a dream. She dreams that real-life people are like people on the television – if you turn the brightness right down some are left with auras, some not. Angie and Billy and Dee all have auras, but her own is insubstantial. In the days that follow, she hangs onto this dream, trying to decipher it, wanting to give it her full concentration. But she can't. Even the empty rooms have listening walls and doors. All around there are people breaking into her attention.

"Ah Amanda," Glynis says. "As you know we're nearing the end of the season and I'm just trying to find out which girls are interested in coming back next season."

"Oy Mand," Dee says. "Did Glynis ask you about next year? I'm definitely coming back. We've had some laughs, haven't we? We must keep in touch over the winter."

*

Amanda walks along the beach. It's a blowy, low-clouded day with sea-spray in the wind. September is near at hand, you can feel it. The sky is filled with the warning cry of seagulls and the waves break with a thunderous pebbly crash on an empty shore. Then there's a lull. The fleecy rush again. Then the lull. This euphonic rhythm will go on and on and on. Down there at the edge, the stones are sucked back with each inhalation and then shuffled about with the exhalation waves, those that aren't more deeply embedded. She digs out one of the stuck fast stones and walks on to the harbour. The sun comes out briefly and lights up the seagulls and her spirits. Jo is here. She can feel her. The stone is warm in her hand and as she makes her way back to the hotel she experiences Jo as her astral self – almost superimposed, but not quite. This is what the dream was saying then – that Jo has a powerful aura. And Amanda's aura needs Jo's in order to shine through. Like a planet needing the light of a star.

Go home. Go home *now*. This is what Jo's telling her.

All the time that Amanda has been down here in Devon, Jo has discovered the Liverpool connection meanwhile, and crossed in the post, so to speak.

The season will end in a few weeks but she can't hang around until then. Tomorrow she will go home.

FOUR

As she staggers along the platform at Lime Street station, one of the first things that catches Amanda's eye after passing through the ticket barrier is the display of books at the newsstand. They are all of the thick blockbuster type with titles in bright-coloured metallic letters and somewhere, on the front cover of each, the picture of a stunning young woman features. One of these would keep her busy for a while. Would kill some, but not enough, time. She is not expected back for another few weeks yet. She could get a taxi home, she supposes, though she doesn't have much money on her. Or she could phone Neville and ask him to fetch her after work. Yes, she'd prefer to do that. Get her bearings a bit. Wander around town. Prepare her self for a home-coming.

She leaves her case in the left-luggage and goes in pursuit of a telephone. There's a keen wind blowing. There's always a keen wind blowing up the Mersey. She looks down and sees tons of cigarette ends squashed between the paving stones. Good old Liverpool.

She finds an occupied telephone box and while she waits in the small queue outside (she has plenty of time on her hands after all) she watches the Liverpool couples pass by. There goes a typical couple. The girl links the boy. Always she who does the linking. She is the chattel, the extra piece he drags along, the piece that has to fit onto him, his arms almost akimbo as he blasts around town like a warship.

Eventually she telephones Neville at his shop. She's

glad he appears unruffled by her return and agrees to pick her up after work. About six o'clock. "If you don't mind looking round town awhile," he adds.

She doesn't mind at all. But first she feels obliged to ring her mother.

"It's me Amanda," she says. "I'm in Liverpool."

"Oh." Her mother is taken aback. "But we weren't expecting you back yet. Is everything all right?"

"Yes. I've phoned Neville. He's going to pick me up later." She can feel her mother's stare on the other end of the line. "I'm going to wander round the shops till then. I could drop in and see Angie…"

"That won't be necessary. Angie came home early today with a migraine."

"Oh dear." The conversation has come to a dead stop. She hates phones. She wishes the pips would come.

When she's finished the stilted communication with her mother, she decides to go to Angie's shop anyway. Large department stores are great time-killers and wonderfully anonymous. It's when she is lurking by the elaborate hats on their polystyrene display-heads that she grows nervous. Each time there's an announcement over the Tannoy she expects to hear her name and a message commanding her to go to the store manager's office urgently. Instead she hears an announcement about a lost child. His description is given out for the attention of all shoppers – aged three, red jumper with yellow teddy bears across the middle, blue anorak, red shoes, fair hair. Answers to the name of Christopher.

She suddenly feels sick and rushes to the toilets. She imagines finding the child in here, crawling on the floor, oblivious. She imagines how easy it would be to steal him. Just like Jo. Stolen, and a new identity pinned on her like a badge, stabbing her in the chest every time she puts it on.

*

Neville is only a little late. When he spots her he plants a kiss on her cheek and on the way home she briefs him about her working holiday. But he isn't really listening. He asks too many questions a second time.

The homeward route offers few surprises: a few more houses bulldozed, a bit more graffiti on crumbling walls. Maybe one or two more shops have opened or changed hands. Nothing much to write home about. The suburban trees look sad and outnumbered by bricks. Maybe it's always been so. Liverpool – they say it's a dying city but it never quite dies, there will always be a resurgence at the eleventh hour. Such is the nature of this depressed, optimistic city.

Picture follows picture, smooth, like television transmission but her mind still feels rocked numb from the long train journey in spite of her interlude in the city. When they arrive home she meekly tails Neville through the side-gate and on through the back door. Her mother is sitting at the kitchen table, cigarette pointing upwards like a pencil; the remains of the summer on her face already fading to the colour of weak tea. She looks up briefly from her *She* magazine.

"Ah, the wanderer returns," she says. "Are you hungry? Your dinners are keeping warm in the oven."

Everything, though so familiar, looms strange. "How's Angie?"

"Still in bed. But a bit better now."

She wonders whether she should give her mother a kiss. Isn't this what daughters do following a long separation from their mothers? Isn't now the time to hand her the gift-wrapped box of clotted cream fudge? But it's right at the bottom of her case. She dallies too long between the two alternatives – to give or not to give – and the moment is duly lost.

She turns to Neville, leaning against the washing machine, his arms loosely folded against his rounded frame. His wiry, kidney-coloured hair is flecked with paint. Neville is handy with a paint pot. He likes to decorate and touch up window frames and doors in his spare time. Painter, decorator, chauffeur, gardener – that's Neville. Perhaps she should give *him* the traditional souvenir for the services he discharges so obligingly. It is for both of them to share, after all. But again she oscillates, now regretting having bought the stupid sweets at all.

"Right then," says Neville. "You sit there and tuck in, Amanda, and I'll just take your case upstairs before joining you."

Oh, and Neville the porter.

*

After eating, Amanda goes to her room which is warm and tidy, even if a bit stale from disuse. Tinker lies curled up on her duvet. She makes a fuss of Tinker and then Angie comes in. They hug.

This is home, she thinks. Angie is home. This is what has slipped away these past few months, this sisterly bond.

She's also bought a box of fudge for Angie. With Angie you don't need to worry when would be the right moment to give. All moments would be perfectly acceptable but she can't give Angie a box and not her mother.

"It's great to be home, Angie. I've felt sort of incomplete without you. Have you felt the same?"

"Well yes." Angie is looking in the dressing table mirror, pulling at her fringe and rearranging bits of it. "But I suppose it's good to grow on our own too. Away from each other." Now she's fiddling with her lip salve, pressing her lips together. "It's a sign of maturity, isn't it?"

To hell with maturity, Amanda thinks, later, as she unpacks her case. *You are the only safety-net, Angie, between myself and madness.*

The two boxes of fudge peep out from beneath a white crumpled towel with Heathfield Hotel embroidered in dark brown stitching in one corner. Amanda smiles to herself as she takes out one box, peels off the cellophane and stuffs herself with Devon confectionary.

*

Two weeks later Amanda sits on the end of Angie's bed. The worst of Angie's latest migraine is over and she is able to chat, although only softly. There's a lamp on the floor and in front of it, Angie's black umbrella is opened out as a kind of a screen.

"It's bad luck to have them up indoors, Angie."

"Only over your head. Anyway sod bad luck. The filtered light makes me feel better."

Angie is going to ask her a favour. This is what she is building up to. She often asks people to do things on a migraine rebound.

"The time has come, Amanda."

"What time?"

"Do you remember I asked you that favour ages ago? Before you went to Paignton?"

"Oh you mean the poetry?"

"I mean the poetry! Billy's insisting on seeing it." She twiddles with the end of a spoke from the umbrella. "He just won't take no for an answer. He says there's no point writing it if it's kept locked away. He says how will I ever know how good it is if I don't get any feedback."

"Can't you just tell him that you do it for pleasure?"

"Believe me, I've used every excuse in the book. It's too late now to back out and tell him that I haven't actually written a bean since primary school."

"I said you could borrow some of mine if you want."
"And you're sure you don't mind?"
"I don't mind."
"You're an angel, Amanda. You'll be doing me such a favour. I'll owe you one sometime."
"I better go off and write some."

She realizes she shouldn't have said that because Angie is looking worried afresh. "You've got some already, haven't you?"

"Well, they're not very good. I've got to be happy with them if they're going to be shown to someone else."

"Of course. Oh Amanda, you don't think I'm awful, do you? It's just that Billy seems to have this image of me as some dizzy eccentric and I feel I have to live up to it."

"Well if he saw that umbrella like that I'm sure he wouldn't think anything else."

Angie laughs. "Amanda, thanks."

*

Some weeks later, Amanda is in Seaforth having spent the afternoon with an old school friend who insisted she come over and tell her all about her time in Paignton. On her way back to the bus stop she coincides with Billy, himself having just moved to Seaforth and renting a partly furnished house which has stood empty for months.

"Come back and see it if you like...have a drink. It's nothing spectacular but I like it."

So, in the last moments of twilight, Amanda finds herself walking with Billy to his latest dwelling. Between the two rows of terraces, at the road's end, a plaintive November wind blows across from the container base. Billy's house is the only one in the road with a door scraped down to the wood.

Billy bangs on the door and a dumpy schoolgirl opens it. "You should have told me you were bringing home

43

one of your girlfriends," she says. "I'd have tidied up for yous." Then looking at Amanda she says, "Fellas. They leave the place a right tip." She then picks up a biology textbook, an exercise book and a ruler. Amanda notices her sleeves rolled back and a number inked along her freckled arm. Probably she will dial the boy's number when she gets home and later the pair of them will drink cider in the park before the youth club.

"See yuz, Billy."

"Tra Trace."

Trace looks at Amanda on her way out. "I hope you never thought I was dead hard-faced saying you were one of his girlfriends."

Then she is gone.

"Take your coat off," Billy says. "Make yourself at home. Just throw that stuff on the floor and grab yourself a chair."

Amanda sits in a room where the walls are saddled with a discoloured rose-petalled wallpaper, the choice of an elderly aunt who lived here before, perhaps. In fact, this whole fusty room is crowded with other people's history: two frowzy armchairs, an oval mirror, curtain-covered tea chests, the skeleton of a defunct bed standing vertically against the north wall – its decapitated headboard leaning in front. Somehow she imagined Billy living in a brighter, tidier place.

Something of the ugly schoolgirl remains. There's still this scent of someone livelier, cheekier, a joker. Amanda worries that Billy will see her as an anti-climax in comparison; someone unable to match the standard laid down by the previous company. It's that terrible situation again, where the responsibility of talking, of entertaining, falls fifty per cent on her shoulders. More than fifty. The good thing about Billy is that he is at least extravert so the responsibility won't increase to hundred per cent as it does when she's with the quieter folk. She can't help but notice though, that she has, even in this short space of time, had a sobering effect on Billy's usual jocularity. She feels the strained atmosphere as he emerges from the kitchen.

"I'll just clear a bit more space," he says, kicking a weighty cardboard box towards the wall. "As you can see I haven't properly unpacked yet." He occupies the other frowzy armchair. "That was our kid. She likes to drop in after school sometimes. Got her own key."

"She doesn't look like you."

"No. She's got our mum's red hair and blue eyes. I've got my dad's brown curls and brown eyes. And good looks!" He gets to his feet again. "So…d'you want a drink?"

"I don't mind."

"Beer? Vodka? Guinness?"

"What are you having?"

"Have what you like. I always keep in a bottle of Mateus Rose."

"A bit of that then."

"Sorry about the mess," he says, as he fixes the drinks. "See that old bed there? I got that at yer old fella's shop."

"You mean Neville's."

"Oh yeah, sorry, that should be yer old step-fella or should it be your step old-fella?" He laughs, and knocks back his beer. "So, how's the poet?"

"Which poet?"

"Angie, of course. I bet she's shown them to you before but I got her to show me some last week. She's been dead shy about them but I've been on at her for ages. They're dead good too, some of them."

*

Just after Tracey went, Billy found himself wondering

what on earth possessed him to ask Amanda back to his house. He'd forgotten just how bankrupt her speech was, and suddenly longed for Angie's company. "I'll just put the radio on," he said, glad of the jolly background sounds of Radio City with its constant flow of chatter and music and advertisements. Anything to distract him from the quiet shadow of Amanda. Then, tiring of the radio he said, "How about an album?"

Now several drinks and records later, he feels rather different. Yes, he misses Angie – they would be fondling and petting in an armchair by now – but he's no longer bothered by Amanda's lack of animation. She sits like a stuffed animal, her thin hair hanging down one side of her face, camouflaging one half of her expression. But even the exposed half gives away nothing. Still waters run deep, he thinks. He's sure he's had this thought about her before. The drink is making him think bold thoughts. Why did she come here this evening anyway? She didn't have to. Perhaps she fancies him – just a little...

If he's perfectly honest, he's beginning to find her slightly alluring, rather than cold; challenging rather than hard work. And challenges can make him feel horny. This minute, he would love to bring her to life, to feel the pulse, the breathing, the ripples. She too can be stirred into motion, can't she, by the strongest undercurrent known to man: the libido, the sex drive, lust, passion, call it what you will.

She never says 'no' to anything. Would she differ in this respect? An inner battle is waging. It wouldn't be fair to Angie, though Angie wouldn't need to know. But Amanda might tell her. Then again, Amanda wouldn't want to upset Angie and, in any case, Amanda doesn't talk much, not about private things. But she might tell Angie things because Angie is a girl and her stepsister. Or it might slip out in an argument. But if it did and

Angie confronted him he could always deny it.

What is he thinking of?

But in spite of himself, he moves onto the arm of Amanda's chair. He fills up her glass, and pretends to discuss an album cover with her. No harm done.

After a while he says, "What about you, Amanda? Got yourself a fella yet?"

"No."

"Well, I'm sure you will soon. You're a nice-looking girl too, you know."

She gives an embarrassed giggle.

"I'm serious," he says, stroking her hair. She doesn't resist which is a good sign, he thinks. She is different than most Liverpool girls he's met, who wouldn't have let him get this far. Liverpool girls guard their bodies well, sometimes it can be like Fort Knox getting in, even with the gregarious among them, especially with the gregarious, until you're going steady with them. But Amanda is a Blundell*sarnds* girl. A quiet Blundell*sarnds* girl at that and he knows what they say about the quiet ones ...

"Amanda? You've definitely got something," he says, as he puts an arm round her shoulder, and lets his hand stray towards her neckline, to those buttons which, in a minute, she'll let him undo...

*

The naked bulb hangs down on a wire as they lie on the floor. The mineral shines on the animal, she thinks. She is going through the motions. It may be a physical act but there are so many mental ramifications, unwritten laws, rights and wrongs, dos and don'ts, where sex is concerned. Indeed sex is fast becoming a bureaucracy. What do other people do when they're seduced? Dee seemed to know what to do. Dee might not be academically qualified but she knew when folk should or shouldn't touch her. "Get your filthy paws off me," she would probably say in this situation. "Your my sister's bloke." Dee would know when was right, and when it was right she would throw herself into it whole-heartedly. Dees carried their confidence to bed with them. Amanda knew she had more brains than the Dees of this world but she felt a sexual dimwit in comparison, never sure when to protest and when to co-operate and usually ending up doing neither. At least when touching her own body, bringing it to pleasure, none of this social communication stuff was necessary...

Tonight, however, she's relieved to have done it. An opportunity presented itself and she took it. So this must be why people referred to sex as 'it'. She has now done 'it' too, which untried, set her apart from most of the adult population. Now 'it' could be mostly forgotten – (Billy used a Durex, so there could be no comeback) – leaving her to get on with her life in peace.

They have been lying here in silence for some time, she and Billy. He smells of Aramis or some old aftershave that Angie once gave him for his birthday. She slips upstairs to the bathroom to wash all traces of it away and when she returns to the fusty room, Billy is lighting a second cigarette. He has given up giving up he says. He's telling her again how rotten he feels for being unfaithful to Angie. "I got a bit carried away," he says again. "It was the drink."

"Yes," she says. "I've had quite a bit too."

"It's probably best we don't say anything to Angie." He has said this once or twice already.

"I won't."

Billy tidies himself up, puts on another record, and sits back in the armchair. "Don't get me wrong, I did enjoy it very much," he says, and within minutes his eyes are shut and he's drifted off. But she thinks on, in this weighed-down room. Something about its historic nature transports her anti-clockwise through the years: the twinless years...

Her mother says her real father, Rodney, is dead. But she knows otherwise. She knows that really he has changed his name by deed poll to Bob Arnold and lives in another part of Liverpool. Bob Arnold has an average feel to it though not too average. These days he shines his blackened hair with oil; shaves his ashen skin with a blunt razor and washes away the surplus blood in chilly water. His black eyes have reached their burnt out conclusion, like gutted houses. He now drives a bus. His passengers receive a cold, punctual service, but they much prefer an erratic service with a smile. You know, with one of those joke-a-minute drivers who switch off the engine while they board at leisure. "Come on, Dawdly Dot, we haven't got all day." That's what the old ladies like. They like travel to be something of a social occasion, like bingo. But in the course of Bob Arnold's scheduled life, he never gives them a second thought, or his slaughtered identity, or the daughter he thinks he's killed. The one he hid in the dustbin. Jo. His brain is like bricked-in dead meat.

One day, when she has the courage, she will seek out Bob and find the truth.

Outside, there's a gentle rustling. Wind blowing the gutter's litter or rain on glass. Inside, Billy's watch is ticking, loud as a cricket. She watches him and as though by telepathic force she makes him move and open his bleary eyes.

"I'm really sorry," he says. "Would you like a cup of coffee?"

"Yes OK."

He staggers to his feet and goes to sort out the coffee. On his return he hands her the cup and says, "D'you know

49

something? I wasn't properly asleep before."

"Weren't you?"

"No. I was hovering between two consciousnesses – try saying that when you're bevvied!"

"You looked asleep to me."

"I was dozing but also very alert if that makes any sense. I was staring at that bed that I bought from your old man's shop. Then I closed my eyes and started thinking of him ... your dad."

She feels her head clench as if by the teeth of some vicious bear. Billy has raided her head. Either that or her mind is an open drawer with its contents spewing down her face. She has to leave. There isn't time to finish her coffee. "I'm sorry," she says, jumping up from her chair. "I didn't realize what the time was. I better be going otherwise they'll be wondering where I've got to."

"You've got time to finish your coffee."

"I've got a bus to catch."

"I'll get your coat then and walk you to the bus stop."

"It's all right. There's no need."

"No, I insist."

Neither of them says a word until they reach the bus shelter which rattles in the wind and then Billy says, "I don't want you to think I make a habit of – you know. I'm dead sorry for getting carried away but – well it takes two to tango, doesn't it?"

"Yes, I know. It was my fault just as much."

"So we're agreed then. Not a word to Angie."

"Well, I'm not going to tell her."

"Good stuff," says Billy, and then they fall quiet because another couple is now waiting at the bus stop. A real couple, the bloke standing behind the girl, his arms round her waist keeping her warm, his chin on her shoulder. The bus comes, and the real couple have a long snog goodbye before the girl gets on the bus.

*

Amanda is glad to be on the bus. She sways into a vacant seat upstairs. Behind her, on the back seat, is a posse of teenagers. She hears their jaws churning gum, hears filtered sniggers, the squeak of their marker pen. A boy vents a loud, coarse belly-laugh but the girls outlaugh him with their blank shrieks. Gusts of cigarette smoke fog the air. The few heads in front of her bounce up and down in time with the bus. Her head is still thick with drink.

The bus is deep into Thornton – it took a different route than expected. Either that, or the drink has wiped out parts of the journey. As she lurches off the bus she thinks that it's just as well she's in Thornton – she needs to walk a bit to clear her head before going home.

After walking a bit, she realizes her head is clearer than she thought. She is able to observe details, like her shadow growing shorter as she approaches each streetlamp until she is able to stand on it; then she watches it expand again. She is happy to do this all the way home but she is disturbed by resonating footsteps, as though down some back alley. Someone is behind her, one of those twerps from the bus perhaps. She stops dead under the violet glow of the next streetlamp.

Nobody passes.

Eventually a dark figure approaches from the other direction and brushes against the hedges. At the point of passing, Amanda makes the mistake of looking into the glinting whites of the woman's eyes. Silent revolvers point at her, holding her to ransom.

She runs until she reaches the Moor Lane traffic lights. By day, this road bustles and clatters and shakes under the muddy tires of cars, lorries, ambulances, buses, which makes the sight of those traffic lights – now flashing out their silent orders to empty concrete – all the more eerie. The amber lights withdraw slowly and two brilliant red ones shine out beneath their black bonnets in rehearsal for daytime. These lights are shining into my mind, she thinks, lighting up the grotto there. It sounds a warm and pretty thought but it isn't. It's a cold, uncompromising, ghost-train sort of thought. Another light is turned on in an upstairs window. There are so many portentous lights – traffic, street, house, car – all surreptitiously communicating with one another.

A Labrador passes, apparently alone. The dog too is part of the terrible conspiracy. Everything is racing. Look at those trees, not waving but beating their arms in fury. From the depths of a black puddle she sees the reflection of wiggly telegraph wires and a slightly dog-eared moon – the brightest ice-blue. Why people say 'once in a blue moon' is beyond her. The moon is often blue. A bird flits across it, like an arrow. Maybe it's her screech owl.

She crouches over the puddle to take a look at her self and for an instant sees not one set of features, but two interlocking, faint and shifting, in the breezy, moonlit puddle. Jo. Jo has come. Jo has come to help build up her defences. Together they can guard their sovereignty. They can patrol each other's body and warn of enemy forces. Together.

FIVE

The family slowly resume their Sunday afternoon activities, post Sunday roast. Amanda remains at the dining room table, watching through the window as a robin alights on the window sill. His entire chest lifts with the song he is sweetly singing. Then he flies away.
Amanda opens her writing-pad. She reads again the letter Dee sent her at Christmas.

Dear Amanda
Sorry I haven't wrote to you earlier. The summer seems yonks ago now, doesn't it? I'm going to my mums for Christmas. Guess what, I've got this new boyfriend called Lee so we're Lee and Dee! Nothing serious. You and me will have to meet up in the new year. I fancy a trip up north. I want to work at the Heathfield again this summer definite. How about you? It would be great if all the old crowd was there again next summer. Anyway sorry this is short. Have to catch the post. Will try and give you a bell over Christmas. Happy Christmas and new year. Love Dee xx

Amanda picks up her pen. It's unlikely that Dee will travel all the way up here, in winter, after Christmas, and completely broke – but Amanda isn't taking any chances. She isn't in the mood for receiving visitors. She's just in the middle of mulling over the best of the excuses she's thought of so far – none of them terribly convincing – when Billy knocks on the window and waves. He sometimes does this on his way to the back door.

"Hi Billy," she hears Neville say. "You've just missed a mean roast beef, even though I say it myself. Can I get you a drink?"

"A beer would be great, ta."

"Go and sit down in the lounge then and I'll be with you in a tick."

"Then I'll tell you my exciting news," says Billy, "when you're all ready."

"Exciting news, eh? Hang on a minute then and I'll round up the others."

When everyone is assembled Billy can hardly contain his excitement and gets quickly to the point. "Well, it concerns Angie."

"Don't tell me," says Neville. "You two are getting hitched!"

Billy smiles and says, "Er no, nothing quite like that."

"So come on…don't keep us in suspense."

"Well," says Billy, looking directly over at Angie. "It's about your poems, Ang."

"Poems?" Rosalind is looking slightly incredulous. "I didn't know you wrote poems, Angie. Did you, Neville?"

"She's a girl of many talents is our Angie. Never was one to flaunt them."

"Well she does write them," Billy goes on, "And very well too, and that's not just the voice of a biassed man speaking. I showed them to this bloke I know who has a poetry magazine and he wants to include some of them! What about that then?"

"Oh you didn't." Angie is looking more sick with each passing minute.

"I thought you'd be made up, Ang. He was quite impressed, honest. But of course he won't print them without your permission."

"I can't." Angie shoots a worried glance in Amanda's direction.

"Oh you must," says Billy. "You can't go through life being too modest, can she, Neville?"

"I'll say not. It's your big chance to see your name in lights."

"And that's not all," says Billy. "This friend of mine – the editor – has also organized a poetry reading evening at the local Writer's Circle and would like Angie to read a couple of them to the group. Would you be able to do that, Ang?"

"I can't," she says. "Look this has all got out of hand."

"Oh you *must*." Rosalind is insistent. "You don't get chances like this every day. I'd be so thrilled if it was me."

"She doesn't like the publicity, do you, Ang?" Neville says protectively.

"A lot of writers don't," Billy agrees. "That's why I'm even prepared to read them out on her behalf if her bottles goes on the night."

"Oh no," says Amanda, and unfortunately she says it aloud. But he mustn't make her soul a public spectacle.

"What do you mean 'oh no'?" Her mother is looking cross. "You should be pleased for Angie."

"Even though the pond is frozen the fish still swim underneath," says Amanda, not knowing exactly why she said it or where it came from.

"Well," says Rosalind. "I think this calls for a little celebration, don't you, Neville? Go and get a bottle of Pomagne, will you, Amanda?"

Angie and Amanda exchange brief looks of disbelief. They're in this dreadful thing together, both of them fraudulent, both of them guilty. Angie has borrowed Amanda's poems. Amanda has borrowed Angie's boyfriend (admittedly without permission) and so now they are more or less quits.

Amanda returns with the Pomagne. There they all are:

55

Rosalind, Neville, Billy – an impassable hydra. Nothing she or Angie says will penetrate their thick skin. As her mother takes the bottle from her she mutters: "Amanda, do cheer up, please. You might at least try and offer Angie a bit of praise and encouragement."

Amanda feels herself tremble. Sticks and stones may hurt your bones but names will always break you. Retaliate quickly with a cutting reply to that bitter remark, why don't you? But anything said after such a delay will sound practised, edited, tardy. Why do you let her get away with it, you stupid bitch? Why don't you tell her you wrote the poems and to hell with saving Angie's face? After all, if Angie was anyone she would have owned up by now.

But where are you going, Angie? Don't leave me manacled to this terrible trio who pretend to extol your merits but are really pouring ridicule on mine. I'll teach them. Watch me.

She steps into her army uniform. This is the appointed day for returning home in all her glory – the day for dishing out surprises. It's an unreliable day in spring. There are dandelions bobbing in the hedgerows while in the town the old people, like the young, congregate in gangs, speaking their private language, their faces washed beige like old newspaper. Flags and home-made banners cascade from windows, from the snowdrop-hands of children, even from the flanks of dogs, and the shimmering throng in the park is elusive, like a water reflection. All eyes to the sky while the parachutists gyrate toward the painted cross on the ground. They never miss the mark. You might even think it a school sports day with the echo of hand-clapping and the sibilant loudspeaker.

From the top of the town the brass band heads the procession. Floats follow, some colourful, some military.

There are carnival princesses in garlands of flowers, there are cadets, and majorettes, unicyclists, and a fleet of customized cars, and more majorettes...now the tanks roll in - robust, proud, macho...

Earlier there was sun. Pale cardigans flapped freely in the chilly breeze but now the air suddenly reeks of rain, the barks of the trees lining the avenues turn a dank black, their vests a pale lime. There's a cloudburst, scattering the crowd amok like marbles. Lost marbles. One of the tanks – *her* tank – slushes through red mud and lies low in the country, waiting for the first signals of dusk. The young, high-spirited soldiers play gin rummy to pass the time.

Under the veneer of evening they surround Atherton House. They have been given their orders, they know what they have to do, but the couple of strapping young men assigned to this task are having trouble with the back door to the house – that last protection against the outside world, and its verdict. But brute strength is winning the day as the door starts to splinter and split, wood and glass soon crunching, as cockroaches are said to crunch, under heavy boots. The young woman heads the siege, her polished rifle strapped boldly over her shoulder. Her parents, her real parents, take a late meal in the dining room.

"More claret, darling?" Rodney asks his wife. "It really is superb – what the devil–?" Her father treats the interruption with admirable sang-froid but soon things will be different. "What is this?" He sees the gun his daughter is brandishing. The other soldiers march mechanically into the room and fall in dutifully behind her.

"Amanda darling," her mother says. "You do look smart in your uniform. The boys too. I do like to see young men fighting for queen and country."

"Those sounds from the kitchen," says Rodney, "like a door being forced open, that was a most convincing simulated exercise. Had us both going for a minute, didn't it, Rosalind? And then we remembered – Amanda's due home today. Would you all care to join us?"

The fools. They haven't yet realized that she and the men have come as adversaries. But they will. Very shortly. Because this is war. She looks straight ahead. The room has always been empty. Her mother appraises the row of military faces, she is beginning to feel spooky about the whole thing, but Rodney is still trying to milk this stunt idea. Then all of a sudden his conscience stabs him in the stomach, he clutches it, falls to his knees pleading for mercy with clasped hands, tears like cling-film blinding his eyes. "It's Jo. She comes to avenge the death of Jo. Spare us, Amanda, for we gave you life."

He has repented, in a sense, so he will die with dignity. Three shots are fired and he crumples to the floor like a split sack. His wife takes refuge behind the tablecloth, her final curtain. Amanda leaves her to pine for minutes, fat pregnant minutes. She ought to do a clean straight job, like soldiers do, but the normally neutral eyes and thoughts have left their ranks. Not three bullets but one, prescribing a slow death for Rosalind.

Rosalind falls, in pain, making death with her husband. Amanda surveys the half-consumed middle-class family spread. She forks up a piece of lamb. Eyes it suspiciously. "Mutton dressed as lamb." She looks over at Rosalind dying on the floor in her youthful frock. Sips some claret from one of the glasses. Fondles the pair of nineteenth century candlesticks with the mid-drip pans. Thinks they must be worth a bob or two. "Do you like them?" she hears a familiar voice say.

Like a drowning man, Rosalind clings onto the tablecloth, as though it were dear life itself. The decanter topples – weeping claret down that final white curtain – and then, at last, the whole sorry display comes crashing to the floor.

"It wasn't for Jo I came," Amanda whispers. "Because Jo is alive... "

In the town it is raining steadily. The formal festivities are over but the crowds still amble around in optimistic mood in spite of the weather. Over by the marquees the quagmire is strewn with shredded rosettes.

"They're a pair of beauties those candlesticks," says Neville. "This man came into the shop the other day and sold me them for a song. I'm telling you I was well chuffed!"

SIX

Angie goes home from work at lunch-time. All morning she wasn't able to concentrate and one customer became decidedly shirty when Angie was flipping through one of the pattern books with her. "I've already told you twice that it's for a child," said the middle-aged woman with hairs coming out of the two moles on her face. "These are for adults." And then she went and short-changed another customer who was, fortunately, very good-humoured about it. But she knew if she stayed at the store all day, a migraine would take root.

It's all because tonight is the dreaded night. It's the evening of the Writers' Circle poetry evening but she has already told Billy she can't do it. She can't stand up and read in front of a lot of professional writers. "Oh get away. I don't think many of them will be pros," Billy said. "Most of them will be aspiring." Even so. He could see she was still not convinced and that's when he offered to read the poems for her. Reluctantly she agreed, but it's all got out of hand, this poetry business. She never meant for it to go this far and now she can't back out. It's not as if Amanda strongly objects either – if she did it would be a different matter but Amanda seems strangely removed from it all. Ever since she returned from Paignton she has seemed permanently distracted by something, locked in a dream. Maybe something happened to her in Paignton, she wonders fleetingly, and then resumes her worrying.

She looks out of her window onto the sedate

Victorian road where it's still all grey, no yellow flowers yet. A wintry wind snatches away dry leaves, in little eddies, and then a sheet of newspaper. Up, up and away it blows, yesterday's news, like a bird, and she wishes some freak current would carry her off somewhere miles from here. She closes her eyes. In ten hours, no eight, it will all be over.

*

They sit in the public library – Amanda, Angie, Rosalind, Neville and Billy – in one of the row of chairs at the Writers' Circle. The air bristles with anticipation. The loud 7.20 chatter peters to a mutter by 7.40 as the organizer of tonight's event launches into his introductory address.

Rosalind, wearing that lemon coat she sometimes wears for weddings, sits next to an unusually groomed Neville. Next to Neville, Angie sits, dosed to the eyeballs, her nerves completely frayed. Billy, on the other side of Angie, has been delegated the job of reading the poems. Amanda, sitting on the other side of Rosalind, notices how she has started to think in terms of *the* poems, rather than her poems. At the same time she's glad to be avoiding the ordeal, the public humiliation. Instead she can sit back and relax, anonymous, while Angie squirms in her seat, takes the flack, puts her soul on the chopping-block.

Three other contributors read their stuff first. The first is a middle-aged gentleman from Lunt, responsible for some tedious epics, but who is, nevertheless, warmly applauded, mainly due to the enthusiasm and feeling in which it is read. He is followed by two retired ladies, the first of whom is the author of some very twee verse about flowers and birds and sunsets. The second lady's poetry is more blunt and witty, belying her rather genteel appearance. She, like the first man, raises a lot of laughs.

She will be a hard act to follow. In fact they have all been very well-received so far by the audience which is, by and large, in the same age bracket as the readers.

Then it's Billy's turn. The organizer of the event, this editor bloke who Billy knows, is looking a bit confused. He was expecting a young woman to read next. Even Billy looks slightly awkward now as he explains the situation: that the writer of the following poems, Angie Slattery, has agreed for him to read them out on her behalf tonight because she is a bit nervous. Billy adds that the poems also have to be seen, as well as heard, in order to fully appreciate the frequent play on words. "Anyway, I'll waste no further time on preamble," he says. "The first one I'd like to read tonight is called 'The Telephone'.

> Telephone telephone
> Someone plugged you in
> To the volts of my heart
> That I may make you ring
>
> Telephone telephone
> Receiver like an arm
> And wire that holds me
> Protecting me from harm
>
> Telephone telephone
> You've been resurrected
> Next time you ring
> We'll be reconnected
>
> Telephone telephone
> With your mouthpiece so black
> When I whispered into you
> Did you whisper back?

You cannot shout, you cannot curse
There is only your refrain
But telephone telephone
Please speak to me again

Suddenly Amanda no longer feels protected by anonymity. The room feels hot but the heat is coming from within. She has become super-sensitive to every sound, each little fidget from the audience, each little sigh. Then she hears nothing except her nerves as they hammer her body, her heart as it pirouettes. She stops breathing, almost, as Billy leads in to 'Twin Souls'.

One tenant
Grew well
In her shell
Of polished wood

But look at her sister
You fractured
Her tough-looking case
You forgot
To mine the ore from her core
The gold from her soul

Grey powder
Dead clinker
Where once there was nut

An empty shell
Knock on wood
No one there
No.
One, there

And one here

A winter stale
As shut up rooms.
Always vacancies at the inn
No departures, no stays
On the road too
Damn ask us
Why don't you?

For years
Your fears
I lived without
Unroofed
By structural damage

A missing whole
Lying in parts
Dismantled
That's me, I laugh
Make complete
This embryo

Our tears
In arrears
By two lifetimes
A pair on the brink

Infra-penny
In for red
Our colours not twinned
Yet

Early daze
Mend your weighs

Divine Libra
These two sides
Balance
We are metric
We have four feet
But you won't give an inch

Don't cry Jo
God's dice
Will draw a lucky number
Next time
See his point of you

Be my guiding star
Let your aura shine
Through the ozone
To my sun-heart

"Thank you," says Billy.

The people clap but they don't understand or relate. She hears one of them say "a bit way out" and her neighbour nodding in agreement. "Not my cup of tea either. I don't like it if they're too obscure."

Her mother, Neville, everyone in the hall, in fact, have pretended not to observe her mortification but they know really, know they are her words. Callously they sat through it, like cats waiting to pounce, their neon eyes sparkling with the knowledge.

Eyes. She wishes on her crystal vision a slight defect, a small fuzziness, if only to blur out the sight of their eyes that drill through her head and activate the red circuit in her face. What gives those organs so much power? They're only a delicate network of jelly and nerve and tissue, if you are able to reduce them to this, but most of the time she is unable to; most of the time she is compelled to take evasive action by concentrating on teeth, noses or ears instead. If an ear cocks in her direction she is happy to lose herself in its silken porchway. But then an ear head on, usually means the eyes are elsewhere anyway.

After the next batch of poems, and under cover of the clapping – this time heart-felt and empathic – Amanda taps her mother's arm. "Can I have the key?"

"Whatever for?" says Rosalind, still clapping away.

"I don't feel well. It's too hot in here. I need to go home and lie down."

*

She hears lively chatter outside the back door and the light flicker on again in the kitchen as the others return. She is upstairs in her room, on her bed, pen and exercise book in her hand. She hears Neville and Rosalind coming upstairs.

"Are you all right, Amanda?" calls Neville.

"You know why she left." There's aggression in her mother's voice.

"Shh," says Neville. "I want to ask her myself." He knocks and comes into her room. "It was a shame you weren't there afterwards, Amanda. Quite a few people came over to talk to Angie."

Rosalind tuts. "She doesn't want to hear that."

"You look a bit flushed," says Neville. "It was a bit hot in the library. Or maybe we were all putting ourselves in Angie's shoes, eh? Anyway, I suggest you get some rest and we'll tell you all about it in the morning."

Amanda stares at them, baffled. "Why do you all play this stupid game when you know they're my poems?"

Rosalind's mouth is agape. "I just don't believe this. She's now trying to claim them as her own!"

But Neville is half way down the stairs.

Rosalind, on the other hand, isn't going to let it drop.

"Why are you trying to upset Angie? You two have always got on so well. Why do you begrudge her a little bit of success, hmm?"

"I don't. But they're my poems. I wrote them." She hands the exercise book to her mother, and pulls out a drawer full of further jottings and shakes them onto the floor. "And here's more."

"I don't believe you. You've just copied out Angie's stuff. That's a wicked thing to do."

"I don't care whether you believe me. I don't care what you think. You let him put Jo in the dustbin. You're just as guilty."

She's said too much. Her mother is giving her a strange look.

"What did you say?"

"Nothing."

"No. You repeat what you just said."

"I said about Jo, that's all."

"What about him?"

"Him? So you pretend he's a boy, do you? Is that what you wanted her to be?"

"I'm sorry, Amanda, I don't know what you're going on about."

"I told you. Jo."

"Yes. You were old enough to remember Joe. You do mean Joe, don't you? The big jolly dustman I went out with way before Neville."

"Yes." says Amanda, though she doesn't remember any of it. Her mother's making it all up simply to cover her tracks but Amanda knows it will be best to humour her while she's in this kinder, more responsive mood.

"They weren't really your poems, were they?"

"Yes," says Amanda, opening the door to let the cat in. "But I really don't mind that much if everyone wants to think they're Angie's." She strokes Tinker under the

67

chin. "I've got more important things to worry about."

SEVEN

Telephone telephone someone plugged you in . . .

Amanda stands over it, shaking, alarmed by its urgency. It might be Jo. She's about to pick up but then she freezes. Most of her old school friends have fallen by the wayside. But what if it's Dee? She now wishes she'd never written back to Dee and posted it off. She can't believe she wrote back, though she did try and keep it casual, remembering to include a list of forthcoming family engagements and holidays, to deter Dee, to make any opportunities for their meeting up look pretty thin on the ground.

The person ringing up, whoever it is, is a pretty determined sort. Someone who doesn't give up that easily. Someone who rings the number again after a break – as if they know. Know that she sits in terror. Answer the phone, Amanda! Answer the phone! But whoever it is finally rings off, the sound dying away mid-ring, and she breathes out.

What if it was Jo?

Her mother dressed only in a bathrobe, charges into Amanda's room, glaring at her, cross as a swan. "Didn't you hear the phone?"

"The phone?"

"Yes, you know, that piece of equipment that people use to speak to each other. Most people anyway."

"I thought someone else would get it."

"Who? Mr Nobody?"

"I thought you'd finished your bath."

"I was calling at you to answer it," Rosalind says, tightening the belt of her bathrobe with an irate gesture. "Didn't you hear me?"

"No," she lies. "If it's that important they'll call back."

"They *did*. They called twice. What's the point of having a phone if people can't get through?"

Rosalind takes out her cigarettes from the packet of her bathrobe. "What is it with you? I wouldn't mind if it was just the once but this isn't the first time." She selects herself a cigarette and wedges it between her lips, giving her a mean edge, like Bob Arnold. "D'you know, I'm getting just a bit tired of your whole attitude." She lights her cigarette and the uses it as a sort of weapon to emphasize her argument. "I mean you're not a teenager any more but you sit about all day doing nothing. Why don't you get in touch with an old school pal or something like most people of your age?"

Amanda shrugs. "They know where I am if they want to contact me."

"How? If you don't pick up the phone?"

At that moment Tinker jumps down from Amanda's desk and plunges her soft head against Rosalind's leg for a while before finding more appeal in an empty cotton reel.

"Ah," says Rosalind, rescuing last night's *Liverpool Echo* from Tinker's antics. "Have you looked at the jobs this week?"

"I can't remember."

"Well it's about time you did," she says. "Heavens above, this time last year you were feverishly applying for hotel jobs down in Devon and your determination paid off, didn't it? I'm not saying you should do hotel work for the rest of your life– " She spreads open the newspaper on the desk and browses through the

Situations Vacant column. "Ah here we are. This would suit you. Clerk – applications are invited from persons who possess at least 3 'O' levels including English. 'The post is based at the Legal and Estate's Department Office at the town hall and the duties are of a general clerical nature'. There's a lot of security in local government. Or what about this one? They want bakery trainees in Southport and there's a number to ring. Well? Are you going to apply for any of them?"

"Maybe."

"God, if I was your age I'd be on the phone right away."

"I'll be bored in those jobs."

"What, more bored than sitting around here all day?"

"I've got 'A' levels."

"So why don't you use them then and find a job or course that matches your ability?"

Amanda shrugs again which seems to annoy her mother no end.

"You've no answer, have you? Well it's got to stop. If you insist on staying at home then you can do some work here. There's plenty of cleaning and tidying and shopping and laundry to do."

Today her mother looks more frosty and forbidding than usual. It's in the eyes. Eyes that know not how to assuage this inner confusion.

If only her mother knew the unfinished poetry in her head. But she knows none of it. Her eyes are losing that fresh, lively look – they're looking tired and yellow and bloodshot. There's a slight whiff of whiskey surrounding her. As she goes to leave the room she says, "Rodney would turn in his grave if he could see you now – just wasting your life."

Suddenly Amanda becomes taut with attentiveness. "You mentioned him."

Rosalind says nothing. She is nearly out of the room but Amanda doesn't want to lose the moment. "Tell me about him," she says. "Tell me what happened to him."

To Amanda's surprise her mother comes back into the room and sits down on her bed. "I've told you all this many times before."

"No you haven't."

"Yes I have. He died when you were small."

"How small? How old was I? How did he die?"

"You were an infant. He was very ill...I don't like to talk about it."

"Why have you hardly got any photos of him and lots of that fat man?"

"You mean Joe," says her mother. "I haven't got that many photos. Anyway, Joe wasn't fat, just very cuddly."

"And what about the other Jo?"

"What other Joe?"

"My twin."

Her mother is pretending to look at her with incomprehension, a clever move from someone who wants to hide all traces of Jo's existence. "Can't we ever have a meaningful conversation without you veering off into the realms of fantasy?"

"But I know Jo was put in the dustbin."

"Look Amanda, I know what you're referring to."

"You mean–?"

"I mean I had a still birth when you were about six," says Rosalind confidentially. "Joe's and mine. Little Joe. You've remembered his name and somehow you must remember me losing him. You must remember me talking about him."

"No."

"It's still very painful for me," says Rosalind. "That's why I don't talk about it. I always wanted a boy...as well as a girl, of course."

"Girls," corrects Amanda, emphasizing the s. "Twin girls. This happened long before."

"Oh what's the point in continuing with this," her mother says impatiently, getting to her feet. "There's no getting through to you."

For a moment Amanda thought her mother was there with her but now it is lost. She is doing her best though to understand it from Rosalind's point of view. She understands that Rosalind doesn't want Rodney's name dragged in the mud, even if he did kill one of her babies by accident, especially Rodney having being a lawyer. Maybe she prefers to believe he's really dead and not driving a bus across Liverpool...

Her mother's fractious footsteps diminish down the stairs. The house judders as one of the doors downstairs is banged shut and then there is the sound of distant tears.

*

Nag, nag. Situations Vacant, clean the bathroom sink, clean the whole bathroom, men are coming to repair the central heating. Make them a cup of tea, white two sugars, talk to them.

Each separate message pounds out with increasing tempo – this way, no this way, anniversaries that way, signing on over there, job applications her, Social Security, tidy the room, feed the cat, answer the phone, the phone, shampoo's running low, we have visitors, visitors, smile and be polite and help bring in the plates. As soon as some jobs are safely cleared away, a whole new cluster rears its ugly head. What would a flat be like with rent and bills and the rest of it? She lives an endless list as it is.

Perhaps she has become that someone else always worse off than yourself. Perhaps it's her turn to look up the local hypnotherapist. Hypnotherapy seems the thing to wipe away your problems as if by magic. Their numbers are always listed in the personal column of the *Liverpool Echo* week after week. But she remembers some caller on Radio City saying how she had paid £35 to listen to this hypnotist calling her parents pigs before the session got under way and not only that but she had pretended to 'go under' because he only had a few moments to spare before the next client arrived. Spiritual healing then. Maybe that would be more suitable. Or meditation. But she doesn't really have the patience for meditation. She wants an instant cure. A cure for what though? A letter to a problem page? No, she doesn't want her problems printed for everyone to see. In any case, the replies never seem to offer a satisfactory solution and sometimes these Agony Aunts bark up the wrong tree entirely.

"You can be my ear, Tinker," she says, lifting the cat onto her desk and stroking behind those cool ears. She runs her fingers along whiskers spraying out like threads of fine wire. "You know how to keep a secret."

*

Downstairs, Rosalind stands at the kitchen sink trying to fill her mind with pleasant thoughts. She sees the garden and thinks of Neville. That's his domain. There's the greenhouse where in summer tends his tomatoes, or there beyond the paved path, on a warm Sunday afternoon, he can be found shuttling between plots of strawberries or marrows or runner beans, patiently pulling out weeds, or further beyond, digging away with his fork, shaking out the worms or the potatoes.

She tries to keep her focus on Neville. Nice Cockney man that he is. She loves him like a brother these days, but his kindness compensates for any other area of her life that may be lacking. Sometimes it seems longer than eight years ago when he rescued her from that slightly shabby life she and Amanda were sharing in Southport.

Office work never suited her but during those blank years between Joe and Neville she had to support herself and it wasn't easy. There'd always been a man to provide for her. First Rodney, then Joe. Unlike Rodney, Joe was a man of simple means, he didn't have two ha'pennies to rub together as they said in those days, and his house belonged to the local council. But it wasn't dingy like Southport. The Southport house had a sort of passé feel to it: of one-time wealth and grandiosity, the upper-crust once lived in that flat, for sure, with servants and butlers and maids. One day she decided she would sell some of her things: her mother's bracelet, her grandmother's brooch, hat-pin and childhood doll. She took herself along to the hotel where there were antique and bric-a-brac stalls and there she met Neville.

Neville, too, came from humble beginnings. He was a widower and a self-made man and, after living with Rosalind and their daughters for a couple of years in a modest semi, he was able to afford something larger, so they moved to Atherton House.

The dishwater runs over the sides of the bowl. Domestic bondage. How does it come to this? How does ambition give way to drudgery? It just happens, she supposes. Romantic notions slip away. But once upon a time she had aspirations: modelling, dancing, acting, and yet Amanda doesn't seem to have any, it appears.

A deep lassitude suddenly overpowers her, places her on a stool, goads her to the whiskey...

Neville returns.

"I've shut up shop," he declares. "It was very quiet so I thought we might go – are you all right love? You look worn out."

"I'm just tired," she says, unravelling her dark hair.

"You've been working too hard, that's your trouble. Why should you do it all?"

"Who else is going to help me?"

"But you've got a perfectly able-bodied daughter at home. Why can't she help?"

"Christ only knows."

"Where is she?"

"Where do you think? Where she usually is."

"Well it's not right, is it? She wants to stir her stumps - sitting upstairs all day, doing Lord knows what. I'm sorry but I can't abide people just idling around."

"Well what the hell can I do? It's like talking to a bloody brick wall."

"Hey, hey steady on, Rose." He squeezes her shoulders affectionately. "Calm down. I didn't mean to upset you. I'm just worried about you, that's all." He takes the glass from her hand and puts it on the sideboard. "You get up late. You drink most evenings. I come in from a morning's work hoping we can have an afternoon out somewhere and here you are drinking again. You're starting to get unbecoming rings under your eyes. Now I suggest you drop everything, put on your face and let's go out for the rest of the day. What do you say?"

*

Later, they say goodnight to one another, she and Neville, at the end of this long day. Back to back, they are as one, from the hips downwards, their legs and feet entangled, but above they fold away from one another in different directions, like a fountainhead. Neville is asleep, venting regular little throaty noises just short of snoring but she is beginning to toss and writhe on her side of the bed, like a noodle crisping in hot fat.

"Shh. Lie still," says Neville, from his sleep, extending a comforting arm.

She wishes sleep would come to her as easily. Yes, they had a reasonable afternoon. Yes it was lovely feeling the fresh spring wind again on her face as they sank their feet in and out of the sand dunes at Freshfields but all day this thing has been loitering on the street corner of her mind. It's the questions Amanda keeps asking about Rodney. As if she's not satisfied that he's dead. Well, he might as well be dead, she thinks. He's dead in her head and that's all that matters. Today, Rodney is vague and fuzzy. Even her wedding day is blurred round the edges. Fancy that, one of the most important days on a woman's calendar, now gone almost without trace except for a few photos at the bottom of the box in the spare room. Her main memory of Rodney is of a serious and polite person, quite an oddity really, and not her usual type at all. But she knew he would make the perfect husband and father, he took his work and family responsibilities seriously and expected her to do likewise. But she didn't. She wasn't ready at twenty-one. Then along came Joe offering fun and a living-for-the-day outlook on life. She loses herself in the lightness of his laughter for a moment. But it was never the same after they lost their love child, little Joe. And somewhere along the line Amanda has absorbed all of this and twisted it round. The thought of Amanda is a sobering one. More than that – Amanda makes her nervous. She's never thought of her own daughter in this way before but Amanda can be alarming with all her questions and curiosity and odd ways. Why, she once thought Angie a bit peculiar with her migraines and jittery gestures but Angie is a breeze next to Amanda and she falls asleep and dreams she is hoovering along the beach at Freshfields but instead of dunes there's a wall. She is stretching the hoover flex along the narrow strip of sand between wall and sea. She is pulling on the flex, trying to drag the main body of the hoover away in time before the next wave but she doesn't quite manage it and wonders whether the wet will affect its operation. No, it seems to be in fine working order; she's now cleared the wall and is on the wide damp beach hoovering up bits of old twig and stuff, presumably from the pine trees. Suddenly she is indoors, winding up the hoover flex. She is in a room which she shares with three children, one of whom is a baby the size of a doll. She asks one of the older children, a girl, to take the baby through to the other room because his neck was so tiny the hoover flex might strangle him. She looks over at the baby who lies in his gift box under his blanket of plastic bubble paper which is about to smother him. She gives a scream that turns out to be only a throttled gasp, stuck in her throat, but enough to wake both herself and Neville.

"It's OK." Neville runs a sleepy hand over her hair. "It's OK, love. It's just a bad dream."

EIGHT

It's the end of March, and already a year since the Article. Jo's article. Today is the day. Today she will speak to her real father who hides behind the Bob Arnold persona. She has seen him several times already at the Ribble bus depot in Liverpool.

Today is the day. Sometimes you just get this feeling about certain days. She woke up this morning and could just make out those undefined sounds beneath the outer quiet. Those air-in-a-seashell sounds, those rattles in the old servants' bell panel, whispering things, about right days and wrong days.

When she is ready, she takes the bus into town and waits. Bus stations aren't the most salubrious of places. They are grim and dank; they have this air about them, this stench. They are untidy, windy places, where florets of litter scratch along the kerb under the boarding bay and trickles of dubious water form little green pools in corners. But it will be worth the wait...

At around one o'clock, she watches as Bob takes his place behind the wheel of a Crosby-bound bus. He sorts out his change, fills out some figures and then allows his passengers to board the bus. Amanda is one of these. She pays her fare but she can't look him in the eyes – those burnt-out black eyes – as he hands over her ticket. She sits downstairs on the left side of the bus and has palpitations all the way home. He keeps giving her glances through his mirror with those eyes that have wiped out a life. Passengers clamber on and clamber off, now they are in Bootle, now Waterloo. They're nearly at their destination. She's suddenly afraid of what to say to him. She's afraid of clamming up; she fears the cold new identity and the dead-meat brain which has bricked off all thoughts of his twin daughters...

The bus jerks to a halt at Crosby bus station and Bob switches off the engine. All the other passengers disembark, while she stays seated. "Thank you," some of them say, and when he thinks the last of them has gone, Bob reaches for his jacket.

Then he turns round and sees her.

"We're 'ere, luv. Crosby bus station." The accent is perfect. She wonders how long it took him, a former city gent, to get it to a tee.

She stands up and walks up the bus. "Excuse me - "

Her father is fatter close up. Once he was thin as her but he's been tucking into busman's breakfasts to conceal his true figure.

"What can I do for you?" He leans back for his Daily and then takes out a new packet of cigarettes from the pocket of his busman's jacket. He winds off the little piece of cellophane, pulls out the piece of silver foil and screws it up. She watches as he slowly takes out a cigarette, shuts the flap and taps it on the box before pinching it between his lips. He has observed this ritual time and time again from the other drivers – or from Rosalind.

"I've come to tell you about Jo."

"Joe?" He says. "Joe who? Lots of Joes around here, luv."

"Jo's OK...Bob."

"Sorry luv. You've lost me...hang on, how d'you know I'm Bob then? Don't tell me. You're a mind reader."

Bob's continuing with the game. He isn't going to relinquish his identity that easily. He's worked hard to get to this point. She blushes and alights. Bob follows behind, stretching up an arm to a button which closes the concertina doors behind him.

"I'm Amanda...Amanda Court."

"Nice to meet you, Amanda."

But Bob is now waving at another driver and goes on his merry way, leaving her to roam – in utter confusion – endless Crosby roads, all dittoing one another. She walks through Coronation Park where she finds a seat to sit and shiver on. A lamppost creaks nearby and the sun keeps flashing on and off. It's because of those great flowery clouds, all grey and pink, the kind you get during unstable weather. When the sun is off, the flesh on her wrists and lower arms becomes a crop of goose pimples.

She thinks about Bob to take her mind off the cold. She thinks about his eyes which, close to, seemed less black than the gutted pits she was expecting. They seemed to look at her with neither significance nor recognition. But he couldn't afford to. *Pretend, pretend, your good name to defend.* It was neither the time nor the place to let him know that she knew about the dumping of Jo in that dustbin. It was an accident, after all, dropping poor Jo on the floor. Anyone can drop a baby, though surprisingly few do. Anyone would panic in his shoes if the baby subsequently stopped breathing and appeared dead. Rosalind thought Jo was dead too. They both saw her turn blue, they both went frantic, they both tried to revive her, neither of them was rational. Bob said he would bury her in the garden but neighbours might see. Neighbours might see and suspect foul play and so he had another idea.

He disposed of her in someone else's dustbin, miles from home, like she never existed, but Jo was found, struggling for air and barely alive under the compost peelings. She was dabbed spotless and adopted, and no one else knew who she was or why she came to be where she was, except the guilty family. The trail went cold, some teenage mother, most probably, but now Jo is grown up and curious, she is back on the trail...

*

As he walks through Coronation Park, pretending to enjoy his afternoon off, Billy sees Amanda, or someone very much like her sitting on a seat. His first reaction is to disappear, not just because she is hard work, or because they slept together a few months ago, behind Angie's back, but because he has been avoiding the whole family since his recent split Angie. At the same time he feels this urge to approach her.

She is clearly in a world of her own because she jumps when he says, "Hi. What brings you out on a day like this?"

She shrugs.

"I suppose you could ask me the same."

Silence.

"I've got nothing better to do," he says, answering his own question. "I've got the afternoon off so I thought I'd go for a stroll. You need the exercise after sitting in a bank all week."

Silence.

The silence he associates so much with Amanda.

The silence of shadows moving across the garden.

Silence speaks volumes, they say.

In silence he thinks about silence. He thinks about words too. Words are just thoughts spoken aloud and silence unspoken thoughts. What makes a person speak some thoughts and not others? And what makes some people keep most of their thoughts to themselves? Shyness perhaps. But what makes some people more shy than others? Perhaps quiet people are those who were allowed to think a lot as children, allowed to dream, who were left alone to let their minds roam without constant interruption or questioning. Maybe talkers are simply blocked-off thinkers.

What a time anyway to be having such thoughts he thinks. Perhaps he's more of a thinker than he gives himself credit for. But he's also a talker. He can't help himself. He grew up with it – the gift of the gab. You can't help it in this city. Liverpool homes are always so full of chatter and that's why he finds Amanda's quiet so disconcerting.

"I'll go if you like," he says. "It's up to you."

"It isn't," she says, her voice inanimate.

"What do you mean?"

"I don't decide."

"Who does then?"

"Everyone else," she says in that way that makes her seem disconnected in some way. As though she's left her feelings at home, under her pillow or somewhere else safe.

"You want to try living your life instead of letting other people live it for you."

"I can't concentrate."

"On what?"

"My thoughts keep stalling. There's so much busy traffic in here," she says, pointing to her head. "I'm a pedestrian in the middle of a huge busy road, stuck on one of those islands and there's traffic coming at me from all directions and I can't cross... "

"I know about the poems," he says.

"Keep stalling keep stalling keep stalling."

"Did you hear me? I said I know about the poems. It's obvious to me now that you wrote them. Listening to you speak just then. Well it just comes naturally to you, doesn't it? Talking in metaphors and that."

"Angie told you. She mentioned something about it..."

"I'm afraid it didn't go down too well with me," he says. "I'm not saying that was the only reason we split up, it just highlighted all the other things wrong in our relationship." He looks down at his hands and starts fiddling with his nails. "I mean she felt a real fraud and everything, for conning me and half the Writers' Circle and I know I'm just as bad if not worse because of, you know, you and me that time, which she still knows nothing about by the way..." He tucks his hands under his thighs. "But it just made me realize that she wasn't the girl I thought she was. I also felt angry that you were done out of the credit."

"I didn't mind. I said she could."

"Well I want to redress the balance. My editor friend is still interested in printing them, you know. His publication has a trendier audience than the Writers' Circle and he desperately wants good new stuff from young people. What d'you reckon?"

"I don't really care."

"You don't either, do you?" That's the beauty of Amanda. The difference between her and Angie. She really isn't trying to do things for effect. Angie sets out to be different, unusual, but not Amanda. Amanda's too busy trying to fit in, keep in step, too afraid to do anything that will set her apart from the crowd. But there's such a thing as being too chameleon which makes her weirder than anyone he has ever known. More weird than any art students or drug addicts who just live by a different set of rules but are normal in context.

He now knows what makes her tick.

It's the bomb inside her.

And one day it might explode.

*

During such an encounter, like the one with Billy just now, she realizes how easy it is to fall back into the reality waltz. She tries to hang onto its tenuous threads but it's proving difficult. As she walks home she hears the chants in time with her footsteps, *Don't look and you won't see. Don't look and you won't see.* See what? It's the clocks. They've just gone forward an hour and now they eat their meals in the new six o'clock light, they can all see the exact tones of their food without artificial light. But that bit isn't so bad, she can make herself a silhouette against the French window. It's when she's outside that she wants to return to winter evenings which protect her like a thick dark cape. She doesn't have that same dread that other women have of walking home in the dark, fearing what they can't see. Hers is the opposite. She fears seeing and being seen – an altogether different and more frightening thing. She hates this time of year. No more hiding in the shadows. A light creeping in at either end, shortening the dark. And everywhere, dreadful eyes.

Don't look and you won't see.

NINE

Amanda fondles the iridescent beads, their chiselled hexagonal sides, twinkling gold, now lime, now ultra-violet. Sparkly Jo colours. She lifts the necklace from the dressing table and the beads splash off the other end, like seeds. Who gave her this small book of souvenir matches skulking behind the shiny picture-cover of a flashy female? She looks a picture of fun and mischief – a sort of dark-haired Dee or long-haired Marjie. And this silver chain she lets coil in her palm like a worm cast – a twenty-first present from Neville, was it? Has Jo got one? Does Jo want one? Jo doesn't need one. Jo shines bright already...

Her alarm clock points to the eleventh hour. Always the eleventh hour. The baby is overtaken – abandoned on the circuit. Baby is left to take a small step on her own. Mother will be round again in an hour or so. But not for Jo. Not the same mother anyway. But the new one who rescued her from yesterday's news, now soggy and grey, from the compost of tea leaves and potato peelings. What happened next, Jo? You would have lived happily ever after if you'd been able to forget you'd been halved. But like half an apple we start to brown and shrivel and we don't last nearly as long than when we're whole.

There's a bell ringing, though no one else seems to hear it. Amanda flies downstairs to look up at the old servants' panel, the bell headquarters, to see which one wiggles, but they are all still. That's because it's a secret.

A whisper just for her. Jo is *here*, in the house.
Shh! Creep. Hush now.
Amanda follows Jo outside.

The flagstones on the patio where they now sit are starting to get brighter. Vague shadows appear. A pair of identical shadows.

Jo!

Amanda, we must be careful not to leave Angie out, she may get jealous of our closeness.

Angie will be OK. Here she comes. Better stay quiet, Jo.

"I'm fed up, Amanda."

"Is it Billy?"

"Billy. You. Everyone. No one listens around here. You never talk to me any more."

"Neville will talk to you." Then I can get back to Jo.

"Phh. I know when I'm not wanted."

I think you upset her, Amanda.

But I want to be with you, Jo. All this time away and now here we are. Together. Let's close our eyes and enjoy our togetherness.

But when she opens her eyes, she finds herself alone. Funny, she thought she and Jo were now inseparable. Outside the greenhouse Neville has his arm round Angie. They have their backs facing her. Is it muffled tears or just low serious voices she can hear?

When they turn round, she sees Neville with his arm not around Angie but Jo, and she is smiling across at her twin. Radiant, rainbow-souled Jo. Amanda needs to drink in those colours to her soul of grey mist. Then they will be a double rainbow.

"Come on, Amanda," calls Jo, running over to her other half. "Let's see who's the best at planting things."

*

Angie sits hunched on the bench, in despair, her

father's arm around her. They are propping each other up, that's what they've been doing lately, acting as scaffolding for one another, preventing the other from falling down. "Why don't you get in touch with Billy," says Neville, squeezing her shoulder. "I'm sure whatever it is can be worked out." She nods, almost from another world. "What about you and– ?" She can see the moisture behind his eyes. "Me and Rosalind?" he says, and then shakes his head. They both know that it's getting hopeless. Neither of them can get through to her. The drink gets in the way. And they can't get through to Amanda. She and her dad need help but they don't know where from, not without the co-operation of the very people who have caused this need.

"Billy always helped because he made me laugh," Angie says, and her father nods. "You need humour in our situation, don't you?" he says, and they both stand up and try it, desperate grins fixed on their faces, as they did once before, long ago when they lost her real mother, her father's first wife. It was just the two of then. They pulled through then and they can do it now.

She remembers the day her father came home with the new lady who seemed so beautiful with her long dark hair and modern clothes, and not unlike her real mother, to look at anyway, it was uncanny, and somewhere behind her a girl was lingering. Being fourteen years old and clearly the older of the two, Angie took it on herself to make the first move, to make the daughter of her father's new lady friend feel at home. They went on outings together, all four of them, to Southport beach and things. "You need a telescope to see the sea here," her father always used to say. "It's such a long way out." Yes, a nice long walk for two girls who were beginning to share their secrets and the discoveries of growing up.

*

Jo smells of crying. She always smells this way these days. Amanda decides to share her Roses chocolates with her. That should cheer her up. Jo loves the nutty toffee ones inside the purple wrappers. So does Amanda. Jo loves all the same sweets as her. And clothes and songs and books and cartoon characters.

She knocks on Jo's door and hands her the Roses. Jo snatches the plate and slams the door. Amanda leaves her to cry.

And waits.

Jo returns later in a better mood.

"I bet you've eaten all your chocolates already," says Amanda.

"No I haven't."

"Nor have I. I bet you've eaten the purple one though."

"I haven't," says Jo. "I'm saving it till last."

"So am I."

"Why can't you be different than me in some way?" says Jo, annoyed. "Everything I like, you have to like. Haven't you got a mind of your own? Your own identity? It's like having this echo all the time. This tedious repetition of myself."

"But I don't want to be different from you. We're identical twins."

"So that's your game is it? Pretending you're my twin? Well stop it. It's annoying."

Amanda has never seen it this way before but Jo has got a point. People fight and exploit each other the whole world over because of their differences but if there are no differences, people will use sameness to pick a quarrel.

"Jo, I'm sorry – I will try."

"For fuck's sake, stop calling me Jo, will you?"

"But it's your name."

It's not working, Jo says. She says they are too alike

89

and that's why they're always fighting. But I want to dress like you, Jo. I want to do all the things we missed out on as children. You're that wonderful extension of myself.

"Give me some space!" screams Jo. "Stop stealing my identity." The whites of her eyes turn pink, as do her nostril edges, always a prelude to tears. "I'm sorry Amanda," says Jo, suddenly putting her arms round her. "Sorry for shouting at you. I just don't know what to do," she says, her face now varnished with fresh tears. "I wish you'd see the doctor."

"Doctor? But I'm fine, Jo. I'm happy. Why should I want to see the doctor?"

*

A few days later, Billy walks with Angie on Hall Road beach. It's hardly what amounts to a beach in the usual sense of the word, it has this slight stench, and there are small clods of oil, caked in sand, but he has a soft spot for it. People don't come here to bathe, they come here to chuck a frisbee about, or to trot along in silence, as he and Angie are doing.

It was her idea. She wants them to make another go of it. "I'm sorry, Billy," she says. "I'm sorry for not being the girl you thought I was." She slips her hand under his arm. "Make me smile, Billy, like you usually do. I haven't had much to laugh about lately."

He feels like a rat. "You don't want to go back with me," he says. "You can do better for yourself," though he knows she won't accept this without an explanation.

"But I thought– " He can almost hear the wheels turn in her head above the roar of the wind, though it's a bright sunny day. "There's someone else, isn't there?"

"It was just the once," he says, glad of the grit blowing into his eyes and the vigour with which their hair is being mussed by the elements. "It was months ago. Before Christmas."

She untucks her arm from his, and stands between him and the tarred sand which eventually joins the water, somewhere down there. Irrelevant water, because it is unfit to bathe in, with its oily deposits. "Who?" she says. "Anyone I know?"

He's looking down, unsure whether the flush in his face is due to the wind or the shame. She's about to throw the name at him but she doesn't need to. "No!" She shakes her head. "You wouldn't. *She* wouldn't." She wants him to deny it but he can't. He's carried the lie long enough already. "I'm sorry," he says. "It was no one's fault, it just happened," and now she is raining him with thumps. "You bastard, Billy Latham," she says, and runs off.

*

Jo appears, a genie in the doorway. She walks to the curtains, tugging them open for dear life. The light smothering the window is dreadful, white as paper. Whiter. Jo makes martyrs of her eyes, letting them suffer that dazzling agony. Jo is like an actress in a dubbed film – her lips dance against her teeth but the words coming through are out of step with the other cacophony. Jo comes over with screwed-up eyes, black cave-mouth wide open, shoulders rattling. Ow! She's shaking me like a stopped clock. She wants a tick-tock response but you make clocks worse by manhandling them. Why does she do this, my long lost twin sister? And where has her sound gone? Can't she see I'm picking up sounds from another channel?

Amanda cries out, "I can't hear you!"

This doesn't go down at all well and earns her a strike across the face. She is seeing another side to Jo. Another side of facing your reflection head on. She suddenly sees what it is like to watch herself. She has projected herself into Jo's point of view, is absorbed by it, but retains her own viewpoint at the same time. It is a fascinating but eerie feeling. Jo is now Amanda watching Amanda. Amanda is watching Amanda.

"There's only one person in the room," she says.

Jo is leaving, red-faced. But Amanda doesn't want her new-found twin to leave so she follows her.

And now they seem to be fighting. They fight as girls with plenty of scratching and hair-pulling and bites and nasty names. Jo will lose. They are both half selves. But their two halves make an unsatisfactory whole, like a split end. Like an apple that can't be put together again once the cut has been made. One of them has to go. It's you, Jo. You'll be compensated generously, of course. You'll win a very different sort of fight in time to come. Be patient...

TEN

Unable to sleep, Rosalind slips on her magenta nightgown and heads downstairs to the lounge. She pours herself a brandy, drinks it, and immediately feels that delicious burning in her gut. She pours herself a second, lights a cigarette and reclines into the settee.

The drink helps her not to think. Or at least to deaden what she does think. For instance, if she thinks about Rodney, which she's inclined to do lately, she never dwells on the anger he must have felt by the betrayal of his wife; at losing his family to the dustman. She thinks only of the indistinct gentleman in his dapper lawyer's suit. She hangs onto that image, pulls it out of her head every so often as you would a treasured photograph, surveys it, it is always the same, perhaps a bit more faded than the last time she looked, then she returns it again until next time. In the mental album there is also a special image of Joe. He is sitting astride his bike with that jaunty expression on his face, like he might crack a joke any minute, the way he did before sadness swept them apart, the sadness of her stillbirth. There are older sadnesses still, but in her mind's album there is a special Baby Joe: perfect, never born, never died, but held just there, sleeping forever, their pearly Love Child...

Before long, Angie emerges through the doorway in a pink negligee, and joins her on the settee. "I thought I could hear somebody down here."

"I couldn't sleep." Rosalind taps the settee. "Here,

come and join me in a brandy."

"I don't mind if I do."

Rosalind sees Angie is red-eyed.

"You've been crying. What's wrong?"

"Three guesses."

Rosalind hands her a brandy. "You weren't able to patch it up with Billy then?"

"We're finished…I found out he was unfaithful to me."

"I'm sorry. D'you want to talk about it?"

"Not really." Angie blows her nose. "Anyway, it's not just Billy, it's Amanda," and though Rosalind's had a bit to drink she can detect the viciousness in the way she says her daughter's name.

"Why what's she done now?"

"She keeps calling me Jo."

Rosalind recalls again her Love Child. *Ah, little Joe bless him. Our little boy. Joe's and mine.*

"Did you hear me?" Angie is raising her voice for some reason. "No I don't suppose you did because you're just too sloshed most of the time to notice. You don't care about the effect it's having on dad!"

"Ah, here's daddy himself." Rosalind lifts her glass to the ghastly-pale apparition just appearing in the doorway, his hair awry, pyjamas creased with sleep.

"Do you know what time it is?" says Neville, tapping the face of his watch. "How many more sleepless nights am I going to get?" He grabs the glass from Rosalind and bangs it down on the rosewood table. "What's it all about?"

"It's Amanda," says Angie.

"She needs help," says Neville. "We all will before long."

"See? Dad agrees with me."

"She's my daughter," says Rosalind defensively. "Do

you think I wouldn't know if there was something wrong with her?"

"Something wrong?" bellows Angie. "She doesn't eat properly or talk properly, she shuts herself in her room with the curtains drawn. You've seen it for yourself."

"She's right, Rose," says Neville, his arm round his daughter and all of a sudden it's the Slatterys versus the Courts, or the Court, since the other Court – the supposed cause of the storm – is, as usual, absent.

"She scares me sometimes," says Angie.

"Scares you?" Rosalind looks incredulous. "How come?"

"I don't think she's at all predictable at the moment. I don't like leaving my things up there with all those dangerous emotions."

"Dangerous emotions? Ha!" Rosalind's laugh is a bitter one. "The only dangerous emotions are right here in this room."

Angie bares her bites and scratch marks. "So what do you think these are then? Love bites?"

"We can't go on like this, Rosalind," says Neville. "It's time Amanda saw a doctor."

*

A white drawer opens and Grandma Court holds out a hand to her granddaughter – a hand smooth, oily, as though preserved in brine all these years. "Jo will be safe here with me," says Grandma. Beyond the curtains the travelling theatre has folded up, moved on to new climes in search of recognition or maybe just existence. They fragment easy, like pencil shavings. Backstage, Amanda is immersed in a perpetual state of déjà-vu…

Amanda Amanda AMANDA! Someone seems to be shouting her name. She finds herself sitting precariously on a piano stool. If she twirled around and around on it, would it add to the confusion or would it have the effect of a double negative and cancel everything out? It's Neville's piano stool. She must be downstairs then, though she doesn't remember coming here.

"Amanda, I said could you please take the cat off the piano. You know how it upsets Neville."

Amanda carries Tinker down. It is easy enough to obey commands when you hear them. Her mother has got the cleaning bug, it seems, if her feverish polishing of the piano is anything to go by. Soon it will be as a mirror. Her mother screws the duster up and leaves it like a dead flower on the piano lid. Her expression is tight-lipped.

"Lift me out some music, Amanda."

"But you can't play."

"Then I'll play without. What's the use of having a piano if it's never played?"

Her mother makes a fearful racket, crashing and banging any old keys like a two-year-old. Tinker's ears bolt backwards and soon she is fleeing from the room to escape the almighty din. Rosalind then becomes more thoughtful. "I wonder if I remember..." She taps out some elementary tunes with one tentative finger. The keys have that wonderful, mournful, out-of-tune sound, like infant school pianos.

"I've never seen Neville play," says Amanda. "Can he?"

"Rustily, I expect. He bought it for its rarity and outward elegance – not for its sound."

"Is he leaving?"

"Let my hair down, Amanda."

As Amanda removes the clips, her mother's hair comes billowing down. Rosalind moves her hands from the keys so that only the after-hum can be heard.

"Is Neville going?"

"Let your hair down, Amanda."

"It is."

"What makes you ask that?"

"Angie said something...the other night, was it?"

"He's given me an ultimatum. To stop drinking. But I haven't, have I? I can't," she says. "Come on, Amanda, let's have some *life* in this house. Dance. Go on, dance! Aren't you young?"

*

That was a good-ish day. Bad days – like today – feature the telephone. Bad days are when Rosalind shouts at her because of unanswered telephones. Phones are such eerie things. Even disconnected ones. Discontinued lines. They're eerie too. Something that was, but is no more. Just the word discontinued makes her bones shiver. Reminds her of Jo. Past continuous – this is another spooky phrase. Something past, but incomplete. Then there are parts of family trees which evoke the same feelings: second cousins once removed. This time it's the word 'removed' that is the key one, and there's also the way some family shoots and branches come to a dead-end. The generation ends there, blocked off, a no-through road. She is one of these: a no-through road. She hears talking coming from her bedside lamp, telegraphic-like. It's Jo trying to communicate from the other world:

Lend
A Friend
Before I go round the bend.

*

Angie passes through the revolving doors of the grand, city centre hotel in whose bar she and Neville have agreed to meet after work. She loves this place, she thinks, as she makes her way to the powder room through luxurious cerise pile; the thick, stifling lights fixed into the ceiling beaming heat down on her as she walks. In the powder room there are plants and soft creamy seats where rich ladies sit to powder their noses or dab some cologne behind their ears and chat about the beautiful ballroom.

Neville is seated at the table in the lounge bar when she comes out. He buys their drinks, they talk about their respective days at work briefly, and then Angie says, "It's so nice to be able to talk properly."

Neville purses his mouth and nods. "A rare luxury these days."

"Dad?" she says, after a while. "Things just haven't got any better, have they?"

"No," he says, the smile sad on his burdened face.

"I've been thinking seriously about what we talked about the other day," she says. "You know, about London. I would really like to go with you."

"Are you quite sure? It's a big step you know, Ang. I wouldn't want to be responsible if it all went wrong. I don't want to drag you away from the life you've got here."

"I haven't got much of a life here…not since Billy and I split up. And I'll be able to find work in London, I've already spoken to my boss about possibilities."

"Oh there'll be loads of opportunities. And I'm sure your Uncle Harry will help you out, if needs be. He's got lots of new contacts for me."

"Well yes…and you've still got some old contacts, haven't you? It shouldn't take you too long to build up your business again. I just think a clean break will do us both the world of good."

"I do love Rosalind," he says. "When she's sober but it's such a rare thing nowadays. I did tell her it was me or the drink. And I meant it."

"Oh you have to mean it," she says, reaching in her pocket for her lip salve and rubbing it along her lips.

"Maybe the separation will shock her into doing something," he says. "Maybe in a year from now she'll be as she used to be."

"You've got to live in hope," she says.

"But she's got to seek help. It's got to come from her."

He's also worried about Amanda, he says, and the guilt he might feel for abandoning her at her time of need. Angie might have shared these feelings too, had it not been for the sense of betrayal Amanda and Billy have left her with, but her father doesn't know about that, no one else does. Everyone else has enough problems of their own.

"We wouldn't be abandoning them, dad. We can support them from a distance."

"I suppose so. And if we do go Rosalind will be forced to face up to things, won't she, instead of burying her head in the sand, and that may not be such a bad thing."

"My thoughts entirely," she says. "But if I don't get out soon, I'm going to go under too, and so are you, and then we'll be no use to anyone." She looks at her watch. "Another drink, dad?"

"I think I'll just have a coffee, Ang," he says, pushing away his unfinished beer. "Alcohol seems to turn my stomach these days."

ELEVEN

It's with feelings of apprehension that Billy approaches Atherton House. The house alone would make anyone feel the same, with its grave face and proper deportment. A house of good character, he thinks, trying to keep himself amused. A house from a good background with an elegant name.

It's quiet, keeps itself to itself, like its neighbours.

You wouldn't even know it was summer in this road except for the trees and flowers. Summer to him, preserved from childhood, means a street full of kids on bikes or roller skates or playing hopscotch, it means row upon row of sheets and pillow cases billowing in the breeze, doors open everywhere, neighbours chatting over fences.

It isn't just the physical appearance of this place that makes him nervous. It's the uncertain state of the people within. But in her recent letter Rosalind told him to call. Any time, she wrote. We're always here, Amanda and I. It's just the two of us now. Neville and Angie have deserted us.

Steeling himself, he rings the bell.

"Billy, how nice of you to call," says Rosalind, immediately putting him at ease. "Come in – or should I say come out."

"I was hoping you'd say that Rosalind," he says, looking forward to an afternoon on the grass in the sun. This is where Atherton House comes into its own, in the back garden it keeps. "It's much too nice to be indoors on a day like this."

"Would you like a drink?"

"It's a bit early in the day for me. But thanks anyway."

"Oh go on, Billy. Keep me company. One won't hurt"

"No, really, Rosalind. I've got my new motor outside. I don't want to be going back to bus stops so soon, no way!"

"A new car? How splendid. You'll be able to take day trips to the seaside and the like."

"That's what I was thinking."

"It'll be great if the weather stays like this," says Rosalind. "Can I get you a fruit juice then?"

"That'd be perfect."

"Go right through and get yourself a deckchair. You know where they are. I'll bring your drink out."

As he folds out a chair next to Rosalind's in the overgrown grass he thinks how he's glad he made the effort to call today. This situation is far from easy, but he's always liked them as a family, and he gets on roaringly with Rosalind.

"So," she says, handing him his drink. "You got my letter then."

"I did."

"Well, I can't say it was entirely out of the blue. It's been building up for a long time."

"But you're coping with everything okay."

"I suppose so," she says. "As much as anyone does in the circumstances."

Billy feels the chill drink falling inside him. "So it's just you and Amanda."

"That's right. Just me and Amanda."

Flies buzz about and Billy wonders if he should offer to do the lawn. It always used to look clean-shaven, done it neat strips, when Neville was here. But he thinks he might offend Rosalind and so he takes a few more gulps of juice and closes his eyes. After a few moments he says, "Where is she?"

"Who Amanda? Indoors."

"What on a lovely day like today?"

"Tragic, isn't it?"

Billy examines his empty glass where the juice has left a thick pretty pattern down the sides. "I got the impression from the tone of your letter that she's still a bit–"

"A bit what?"

"You know…withdrawn."

"Oh, did I say that? She's just got out of the habit of mixing with people, that's all."

"Well…now that I've got my new car I thought she might like a drive out somewhere…you too, of course."

Rosalind swishes her bare foot through the grass. "That's a super idea, Billy."

He puts his glass down and it almost gets buried in the deep grass. "Would she mind if I went up to see her, d'you think?"

"You do as you think fit, Billy."

He's worried he may offend Rosalind by venturing indoors. She may be thinking that, having dispensed with his dutiful social call with her, he can now get on with the real reason for his visit: seeing Amanda. But nothing could be further than the truth. Amanda, if anyone, is the one he's duty-bound to see, he thinks, as he creeps up the stairs to her room and knocks on the door.

She takes her time to answer. When she does appear it's with pale indoor skin and uncoloured eyes – narrowed to reduce the excessive light.

"Hi, only me," he says. "Is it OK for me to come in?" He then realizes she's still in her nightdress, long and creamed with age. "Oops sorry, you're not dressed."

She moves aside anyway.

"Hope you don't mind a visitor."

"I'm not in hospital," she says in that slow stony way of hers.

"No," he laughs, and feels the only way to survive is to escape into the jocular. "In hozzie you'd have the company of other patients and dedicated nurses with cheerful faces and bright flowers."

There is the familiar silence. He starts to wander round the room as a distraction from the heavy hush. He picks up the iridescent beads from her dressing-table and shuffles them in his hand like dice. "Mm. Pretty."

She says nothing as he replaces them on the dresser, meeting as he does the eyes of a child in a small-framed photograph. It must be her, aged eight or nine, smiling. "D'you remember when this was taken?"

She holds it between unsteady hands, it wobbles, then drops, smashing as it hits the floor.

"Oh sorry I thought you had hold…here let me…" He bends down to clear up the largest shards. "Are you OK?"

"I feel…a bit off balance."

"You need to get out more. That's why I've come today actually. To ask you something."

She frowns, but says nothing.

"What would you say if we went out somewhere, you, me and Rosalind?"

"No thanks."

"Oh I don't mean now, this minute. I mean this summer. We could go to the sea, the country, anywhere you like. I've got my new car – it's really smooth and comfy."

"I don't know."

"You never know, you might even enjoy it."

"I'll have to ask."

"Ask who? You're a big girl now. You don't have to

103

ask anyone. You're mum's all for it."

"I'll have to ask Jo," she says again, lowering her head like a sleepy flower.

"Who's he when he's at home?"

"She's my twin."

Billy looks uneasy. "Your twin," he repeats.

"She left me. We had a fight and I stayed here."

"I'm not with you."

"She's not dead. She's white spirit. That was the deal." She smiles a private, inaccessible sort of a smile. "She's with my grandmother. She's a star. I can see her on clear evenings."

"Amanda?"

"I didn't hurt her. I didn't."

"Er no," he says. "I'm sure you didn't."

"She wouldn't come and see me if I'd hurt her, would she? She's happy. She looks after me and I look after her."

"Amanda? Have you been dabbling in something?"

She glowers. "It's white spirit. They're not listening."

He knows he's lost her. She has all the self-absorption of mental illness. Not that he's ever met a psychotic person before, not to his knowledge anyway, though he's read about them and seen them in films.

"What do you get up to up here then, all on your own?"

"She's my twin. I've grown up without my reflection."

He realizes he is utterly defeated and gives up trying to enter her cracked-mirror world.

"Without my reflection," she says finally, before breaking off concentration completely. He slaps his hands on his knees and gets to his feet, wondering why he didn't stay in the sun and the long grass with her boozy mother.

As he closes Amanda's door behind her he catches a brief flash of Rosalind's hair at the bottom of the stairwell and has this uncomfortable feeling that she's just this minute fled down there; this feeling that she may have been up on this landing a moment ago, listening.

When he joins her in the garden however she looks deceptively calm as though she's been lying here, flat out, all afternoon.

"Rosalind," he starts to say, as she plays with the straw in her glass. There are bubbles, as though it's an innocent children's drink, soft and fizzy, but he knows there's harder stuff in there.

"Rosalind, I'm worried. "He sits back down in his deck chair. "Very worried."

"Did she say she would come out somewhere, Billy?"

He watches as the gassy bubbles rise to the top of her drink. "I think she's very ill."

"She'll be OK. If she doesn't want to come, we could always go on our own. Just you and me."

"I don't know how to say this," he says, looking down at his interlaced fingers. "But have you thought of sending her to a specialist?"

"Oh, not even a doctor now but a *specialist*."

"She can't go on like that, Rosalind…"

"You mean a psychiatrist, don't you? Well just you listen here, Billy. No daughter of mine is going to see a trick cyclist. No way."

He is silent for a few moments and Rosalind uses it to return to the subject of the car. "Has it got a fold down roof?"

"No." He finds her remark somewhat callous in the circumstances. "Sod the frigging car for the moment," he says, and is immediately ashamed for having been this rude. He doesn't like using bad language around Rosalind. "I'm sorry…I was just trying to think what's best for Amanda."

"She's OK. She just wants to be left alone."

"I'm just concerned about her, stuck up there on her own and still in her nightwear."

"So she's a bit quieter than other girls. So she likes to be on her own a lot. Is that so strange?"

"It's not just that. I mean you must be worried yourself, otherwise... "

"Otherwise– ?"

"It's nothing."

"No come on, Billy," she says, taking out her straw and sucking on the bottom end, as if in kindergarten. "I can take it."

"Look. I wasn't criticizing you, I just thought that maybe your drinking has got something to do with Amanda." He levers himself up from the chair. "Anyway, I think I better be making a move. I've said too much as it is."

"No please stay, Billy. I'm sorry. Stay a bit longer. Don't let's argue."

"It really is time I was making a move," he says. "But I will be back soon to take you both out somewhere, I promise. Southport or Morecambe or anywhere else you fancy."

"I shall look forward to that, Billy," she says. "I'll tell you what. Why don't we both go and talk to Amanda about it, just briefly, before you go?"

*

After Billy left her room, Amanda watched the closed door for a while. People move into the room, make noises, and somewhere in the hazy labyrinth she recalls you make noises back to them. But there's something wrong-sounding about her sentences these days – they don't always sound quite right, like split infinitives. But when the people come they breathe a different sort of life into her just as when they leave they take it away again. But it's nice when they've gone because it's far easier to sink back into the depths of the ocean-bed than fight and flounder under its silty surface.

She heard talking in the garden. Talk of taking her out. Southport. Morecambe. The countryside? She can't hear much up here. Maybe they said none of it. Bumble bees come and bash against the window...

They burst into her room again scattering a train of questions. The splinters of glass are trodden further into the wood part of her floor, like crushed sweets. Then they go. She hopes they won't return. She locks her door anyway.

Later Rosalind comes again. She comes on her own. She is outside the door, banging. She's come to claim the darker twin, the planet who only reflects a dim light from her central star. The dark twin is a sitting duck. What should she do? Escape through the window? If only Billy were still here. She's safe from Rosalind when there's someone else in the house but once alone, Rosalind's out to get her and none can save her except...

She looks at the lamp. Waits for a message from Jo. None comes but the banging subsides anyway.

She flicks back the curtains and sees the light folding back into dusk. There's a black cat slinking off in slow motion, surrendering to Tinker. Intermittently the intruder turns his head back to make sure he isn't being pursued. Am I safe? The question is written through his velvet anatomy. Hey black cat – I'm an intruder too.

On this side of the window, moths are roosting in the last surviving light. How did they get in? Or are they always here, on the skirtings, in the cracks between the floorboards, waiting to converge on the evening gathering. And where do wasps go at night? And birds when they die of old age? And where does all the false piety in the world come from and where will it end? Perhaps she's inadvertently blackmailing God into meeting her deadline. Deadline. That says it all in a way. They slice a child's head off. The Sue Veneer they brought back from Crete. The words aren't sitting well with their next-door neighbours any more. Hasn't she had this thought before? It's got a familiar ring. Like the conspiriters who are after her. Her thoughts are like beetles huddled under a stone and if someone should lift the stone all the beetles would run off in different directions. If she could only keep the stone down she would be all right.

There's a baby in a hearse but Rodney looks right through it. Absent pupils, and now the banging has started up again. She's getting very scared now. She will have to barricade herself in – but it's too late. The door has swung open. She closes her eyes and her ears and tries to wear her Do Not Disturb face.

"Leave me alone," she shouts as Rosalind shakes her.

"I've forfeited a life," she says, and Rosalind shakes her some more and yells, Shut up! Rosalind takes hold of her arm and hoicks her down the stairs to the rest of the house which looks strange, like when you return from holiday. Holidays – now there's a thing of the past.

"Sit down," orders Rosalind.

"What's happening to me?"

"There's nothing wrong with you. You have the power if you put your mind to it."

"Don't you understand? I don't own my mind any more."

Rosalind pours out drinks for both of them. "Please try, Amanda. For my sake," she pleads. "You don't want to be sent away, do you? Of course you don't. And if there is anything wrong, I'll look after you. You do understand, don't you?"

"I just want silence...in my head...to be left alone."

"I know you do," says Rosalind, almost

comprehending. "I know. And together we'll sort this out."

"But there are ghosts in the house," she says to her mother, afraid to look up at the bell panel, where things jiggle and send messages that only she can read.

*

Somehow, sometime, she manages to escape back to her room, her aerie, where it's safe as a womb. But really there is no need to fear Rosalind because inside Rosalind was her first home. Together they were there, twin heads in the womb, she and Jo, the symbol of Pisces, two fishes nose to tail, completing a circle. *The* circle. She looks at the lamp. Switches it on.

Fire
Of desire
Inspire me
From the mire

The telegraphic voice of Jo. The mire! Something's gone wrong. Jo is in hell! But surely not. Surely Jo has the better deal. Jo is the star put back in the sky.

She throws open the window to see if any of the stars are out yet and a farm of moths and long-legged insects stream through it towards the lamp...

There's only a small ribbon of night before the daylight returns. The swift navy blue flaps like the shadow of a giant bird's wing on the curtains. Long long lightness follows dusk interrupted only by the ghostly ring of unanswered telephones. There's usually a lilac intermission between the white and the navy. Summer nights. Day after palindromic day trailing behind her like an unworn veil...

She is the odd one in. She mustn't go out. Not unless it's absolutely essential. She might ooze into the atmosphere. Infect the water. Damage the ozone with her poison. When will the world realize? The epidemic is mushrooming, like a cloud. She must stick to the quarantine. There'll be a nuclear war. God's way of destroying the earth and starting again, like Noah's ark, but Jo at least is safe somewhere else in the solar system...

No thanks, Billy – can't come out today. Another time maybe, though no time is safe. Your signing on time again. What *again*? This means time for a walk, time to enjoy and fear the walk. Fear it because your thoughts race ten times faster than your footsteps. Because you might be winked out on the way, like a burnt-out star, a black hole in the making. Enjoy it because it reacquaints you with those near-forgotten colours and smells and faces which tide you over for another week, and provide you with fresh pictures to stockpile in your head...

Here is the road to Liverpool and the scare is on. Though only ten steps from kerb to kerb, there is the road in between. Past the school of motoring and into the employment office and join the end of the queue to box 5.

TWELVE

Amanda sits with her mother and Billy in some elegant Morecambe tea rooms with decorative cream tablecloths. Posies of tourists amble in, unable to resist the lure of something served in traditional English fashion, especially when the weather turns wet. Rosalind orders three coffees. When the tray arrives she pours the bitter-brown liquid, adding a coil of cream to each, before stirring away the pretty trickles. Amanda stares into three rotating beige pools.

Rosalind looks towards the vapour on the windows. "What's happened to all this sun they promised us this weekend?"

"It's only a shower, Rosalind." Billy, always trying to look on the bright side.

Amanda tries to listen but she is losing concentration. If only she could concentrate on each raindrop. If only her thoughts didn't keep derailing. They will have a nasty accident next time they drive over the black ice. The axle has gone. Once we find the axle the wheel can turn round again. Maybe it's under the chair. Black polished wheel-back chair. Right up Neville's street.

Billy is looking at her. "Your coffee all right, Amanda?"

"Yes."

Something to do with cars. Oh yes, the axle. Year of the car or car of the year. Cars are part of it. The poison. The hyperdwale. They screwed a virgin mind – devoured it like badgers in the dark.

"Um, the ladies are down there and the first door on your right."

She feels dizzy as she walks, just as Bob Arnold must feel every time he drives that bus. What does everyday time mean to the likes of Bob Arnold with his second face? Time means nothing. Time is dehumanized into its parts. Minutes swell, peak, expire. Swell, peak, expire. Day in. Day out. Remember that...

When she returns from the toilet she sees her kingfisher, sitting outside the window, she sees it turn into a huge black crow.

"Oh I almost forgot." Rosalind is opening her handbag and fishing something out. "This postcard came for you this morning, Amanda. From your friend Dee."

She takes it from her mother and surveys the picture on the front, divided into four segments. Each quarter containing a miniature shot of Devon. She was at her happiest at the Heathfield. But only in April when it was just her and Maude and she had the bridal suite privilege at the Hacienda. She recalls the gold taps. Making them gleam. But Marjie had to go and spoil it, shaking her tits in on it. Their faces form a colonnade – Marjie's, with her sardonic eyes, all dark and tarry like marmite, now Dee's, Angie's, Bob's, Jo's. Amanda passes along it and inspects them. A face is autobiographical, isn't it? Bob's features have the tell-tale stamp. He's afflicted with the same malady. The hyperdwale disease. The sins of the fathers. This is a glass doll – if they smash it they will have to carry my grains in a coffin. I can't think any more. The metal detector always extracts the scraps.

"Well? Aren't you going to read it, Amanda?"

"Later."

Because now is oppression.

Oppression
Suppression
Repression
Make depression

Poetry-head.

There is Rosalind. There is Billy. Swallowing the sediment of their coffee. We are an isosceles triangle. They balance, I don't. Or maybe this is a scalene thing; none of us balance but we somehow stick together. But I hope they'll leave soon. There's nothing worse than being cornered at a table with four eyes always vigilant. There's no escape by shifting your body sideways, or by retreating into alcohol, or low lights. No sun even, to make a silhouette of my face.

It's Rosalind's turn to pay the ladies' a visit. When she is gone Billy says to Amanda, "It's brightened up slightly out there. You ready for a nice walk or something?"

"I can't go."

"Well we can't spend the rest of the afternoon in here."

"I can't go on."

"Would you rather we went home again?

"That came in from the outside," she says.

Rosalind returns, and says with forced enthusiasm, "It looks as if the rain's eased. Should we make a move?"

"Yes, let's." Billy speaks with the same sort of false jollity. "I'll just pay for the coffees."

"No, let me." Rosalind and Billy continue their moral tussle for a couple of minutes about who should pay until Rosalind capitulates. "OK, you win, Billy," she says, and then turning to Amanda says, "What do you want to do now? Should we look round some gift shops?"

"I don't mind."

"For goodness sake, make a decision for once in your

life."

"I'll tell you what," Billy says, quick to intervene. "Let's take a quick browse round the gift shops first, then hopefully the sun will be shining and we can all go down the beach."

"Oh well done, Billy." Rosalind laughs." Thank goodness one of us is decisive."

*

They each sit in a deckchair. They have done the gift shops and Rosalind is examining her souvenirs – in particular some tiny glass animals she fell in love with. The sun has stayed out, as Billy said it would, though it's not very warm. Amanda sits nervously, worrying about the disease she thinks she'd got. The deckchair attendant will never know when he next loans out this chair. Is it fair to pass on this hyperdwale, silently, invisibly, to unsuspecting bathers?

"We can't stay here," she says.

Rosalind has developed a way of ignoring her, though Billy hasn't reached this stage yet. "D'you want to go now, Amanda?" He asks his question across Rosalind who sits between them and which makes Amanda say, "She always has to be the centre of things."

Rosalind leans across to Billy and whispers something which sounds like "humour her".

Amanda decides to ignore her. She looks to the sky, now radiant with sunshine, not a cloud to be seen anywhere. It will stay sunny now, right through till sunset. But sun and warmth spread diseases. Everyone knows that and this is a most lethal variety. She feels frightened and exhausted and confused. They mustn't see her face or they might change it extra-sensorily. The sun is making her sick. She picks up her cardigan and wraps it round her head, Moslem-style.

Billy says, "You've got to watch that wind. Are you

getting burnt?"

"They're coming in at the sides."

She can't quite understand why everything she says silences Billy. Perhaps she's kaleidotalking again. He offers to buy ice creams.

"Billy's brought you here today especially," Rosalind says to her, while Billy stands in a swelling queue. "You could at least show a bit of gratitude."

"I'm not feeling well."

"Fine. Do you really want to see the doctor?"

Amanda says nothing, afraid that it will be the wrong thing. Talking requires thinking and thought tires her out so much, trying to make sure it all comes out arranged, and in the right order. It's Rosalind therefore who speaks first. "Billy's hardly moved in that queue," she says, after a while. "Everyone else seems to have got the same idea all at once."

"My postcard. Where's my postcard?"

"I gave it to you in the café."

Amanda dips into her pocket and pulls out something crumpled. She turns it over and reads it.

Dear Mand, must be a sucker for punishment coming back here! Worked off me feet but having a great laugh. Even better than last year. I've met a hunky KP called Trev but still clubbing it with the girls sometimes. Great new club opened. Most of the ole crowd back this year. All asking where yoov got to. Hope everything OK. Havent heard from you for ages. See ya. Luv Dee xx.

THIRTEEN

The hours for Rosalind are supped up in a haze of whiskey or gin or whatever is to hand. It helps keep her memory lens out of focus – the way she likes it. She rarely ventures back beyond the point marked Joe, though very occasionally she will find herself standing at the signpost marked Rodney which points to that misty terrain behind. She knows if she goes down that route and keeps on walking, part of the mist will clear. But she doesn't want it to clear. Not yet. Perhaps never. She knows what is waiting there; what will be revealed. Usually if she gets as far as the sign marked Rodney she can go no further. She has to turn round and go home again, back to the safe lands of Neville and Angie.

Sometimes she dreams, or maybe it's a walking hallucination, that Amanda is taking hold of her hand and dragging her back through the fog to that place, that hidden place, where the Truth lies. Where all the answers lie. But she isn't ready. Not like Amanda is ready. Amanda has been ready a long time...

She and Amanda each occupy their different worlds where they are sinking in their own separate stupors. And when she is in danger of focussing a little more, Rosalind drinks a little more, and then the blur comes, and everything is OK again. She will come to at some unearthly hour shivering in some wretched position on the settee with a painful, delicate head and a raw dehydrated throat. The lights will be full on, the world in bed asleep, and she will crawl into bed knowing she won't rise much before noon and the telephone will ring on and on and so it goes on...

*

In Amanda's room, a bee hums. She can almost see its transparent, rainbow-ridged wings. She tries to keep the image of the bee in her head but it isn't a bee at all. It's a telephone. Three or four minutes of unending ringing.

She curses Mr Bell for his horrid invention and steels herself to face the extension in Rosalind's bedroom. But the tone is regular here, no increase in loudness as she opens the door. Ah! The bell-switch is off so that Rosalind's sleep won't be disturbed. The noise must be crooning from the voice box downstairs in the hall. She starts to descend the stairs shakily. At least today's models are far less awesome than their parents. She remembers one such example that sat like a scar against the wall of the dank Southport home she shared with Rosalind in the days before Neville. Sat grimly on its dais waiting to chant its one and only spell and when you lifted its lid and spoke into its mouth it extended a claw to your jugular vein. A claw, in similar style to those black bonnets which cover the top eyes of traffic lights. Or maybe each is a lid or a lip to hood the most dangerous eye or mouth. Or hoodwink. And it had a body, narrowing sharply at the neck, from which rose a pair of monstrous Texas longhorns. *But never fear,* the descendants have neither claw, nor physique, nor hideous antler-cradle – just two little black buttons. Innocuous little buttons which will themselves become obsolete before long with the coming of the press-button age.

She's nearly at the bottom of the stairs. Oh come on, the hall should be a booming belfry by now – she's standing at arm's length from the offending monster. So why the fixed volume? Who devised this trick? Well, there's only one thing left to do now – sabotage it at source. She cups the thing in her hands, her trembling hands, or does it have a pulse of its own? She carries it up one, two, three stairs, as far as the lead permits, and then, in a kind of accidentally-on-purpose operation, drops it down the stairs. Bump, tinkle, bump, tinkle, hello? hello? clank – the silly receiver is now dangling in vain between banister posts, like a miniature suicide.

What? Still no end to the bur-burr noise, ringing with rekindled fury from the vaults of somewhere? She runs upstairs in terror to her bedroom, blocks her ears, buries her head beneath copious padding, turns her radio up full blast but nothing will dam the current of ringing.

They congregate again, bending over her like weeping reeds. Does it puzzle them to think a telephone has been deliberately taunting her with its rhyming echo for twenty-four hours or a week? Perhaps half a lifetime?

*

The ringing has stopped. She doesn't know how but the silence is ghostly, deafening, wrong. Perhaps the ringing served a purpose. To protect her from the spiteful words of Life. Or maybe it was Jo, trying to get through. Why did she ever want it to stop? You got used to it after a while, like a lawn mower or distant roadworks.

She puts new words to an old poem.

Telephone telephone
Someone plugged you in
To the volts of their heart
That they may make you ring

Telephone telephone
Are you resurrected?
I don't like you
Quiet and disconnected

Telephone telephone
Receiver like an arm
And wire that protects me
From every living harm

Telephone telephone
With your mouthpiece so black
When I whispered into you
Did you whisper back?

You cannot shout, you cannot curse
There's only your refrain
So telephone, dear telephone
Let's be friends again.

*

The last thing she can remember before being here, in this new room, was a sort of dream about steps. Each one cold, like a slab of wet fish, and smelling of cat piss. She was dropping into some underworld. She held on to icy tiles with faint honeycomb cracks and the smell of stale disinfectant and old shit made her retch. She remembers reaching for a sink and the icy cracked tiles began to fold in on themselves like a collapsing card-tower, burying her in blackness.

Why the toilets? To escape the telephone?

But within these new walls there is no backchat, though there is time. She doesn't know how much. The room is novel. How many nights has she been lying supine beneath this low, bare ceiling, grey as an overcast sky? Perhaps this is her first night here or her first night of reality. Where is she anyway? The drifting medical scents are a big clue. Surely her mother didn't bring her here. And what is the nature of her crime? Remanded in custody, waiting for them to dream up some charge. She thinks she knows what it will be anyway. *You are charged under The Mental Health Act 1959 with not being able to cope with everyday life.* Or something like that. They will back each other up of course. There is safety in numbers, in positions of power. In unanimous, unchallengeable fob-offs. Their prerogative.

It looks cool and dark on the other side of the window and she senses the year has past middle age. In the room itself she discerns a few elementary shapes: the bed, the chair, the low bedside table. She's certain there were people around her, earlier, in beds of their own, and people discussing their mothers and husbands and bosses in a group in some other room. It's coming back. Why have they transferred her? Why is she now on her own? What has she done/not done? How many new brands of pills have blasted her head; latest hypodermic needles pronged her? She must be awakening. But it's difficult to feel real. She must be a ghost then. Or a fantasy or a spirit. A weightless form that can surely float through hospital doors, unseen, home. Home? Where the heart is. All you do is locate the valve, (and she's in the right place for that), and then you're home.

The blankets are heavy. It takes all of her effort just to push them off, and stumble out of bed. Her body is reluctant to float or sail and she abandons the spirit idea. A metamorphosis then. Perhaps they possess powers; perhaps they have some scope on either side of the door.

We'll see. We'll see. She takes a chary footstep. Then another and another. The door is a solid wall against her forehead but it opens easily in spite of the faint push. So they haven't locked her up. So they have no objections to her poison oozing under doors and spreading like an epidemic through the hospital. Such negligence! Uncanny how her thoughts still move along the same grooves. Ha-ha! One nil to Miss Caught.

In the stillness of the corridor a dim light shines. This is a hotel surely. Any minute now Dee will pop round a corner with her bucket and hoover, laughing her gurgly-water laugh...

But someone is coming to rupture the peace – a stout woman with floppy sanguine cheeks, waddling like a penguin. Glynis the Welsh housekeeper? Whoever she is, this woman has very little in the way of neck and her breathing is loud and laboured. Her movements are imperious but her weight slows her down and Amanda, even with her paralysed thighs and wobbly ankles and helium-brain, has a good head start. She vanishes into the sluice where she finds protection amid the clutter of dirty linen, skips, bedpans, dripping taps, cleaning materials. When she thinks the coast is clear she shambles her way to the staff toilets where she hopes for safety, immunity, asylum! In the cloakroom there's a small wooden table which she drags into the toilet before bolting the door. This double protection will provide a sufficient barricade against any officious night staff. Coincidence probably brought out the penguin-woman and she will have, by now, pursued her business elsewhere.

But before long Amanda senses a silent brigade assembling on the other side of the door as she sits on her little table dangling her legs. War is declared early. The imploring, the rattling, the relentless tattoo of fists on the door – they are all terrible sounds. How trivial this scene must look to God; to those souls who have passed on to Life Eternal. Why can't these medics have a few revelating seconds into the absurdity of this situation too? They are in bedlam because of one locked door behind which is trapped one sorry sight. They have lost the meaning of life for sure. She climbs off the table and props herself against the far wall of the toilet. It is cold and hard as marble. She's ready for her attackers for it's better to be forearmed in a mood of antagonism than swallowed in a state of compliance.

Suddenly her will deflates and she falls to the floor in listless defeat, huddled between the bowl and the wall. Standing vertically against the pipe, the toilet lid is a large ace of spades. In the next moment the feeble lock shoots off, the table makes a hair-shivering scrape across the floor and a small phalanx of nurses arranges itself on the other side of the door.

She hides her face in her knees.

The hospital junta looks down on her, powerfully silent.

"I can't sleep," she explains, suddenly defensive, and reddening with embarrassment because she too has now been drawn into the trivia. The stout sister discreetly waves away her colleagues, now that the situation is under control, and holds out a matronly hand to Amanda who accepts it humbly – relieved as she is to be absolved of her abortive wanderings.

"Everyone has their off nights, you know," the sister says, in reassuring tones. "I have my fair share, I can tell you. Now we'll give you something to help make you sleep and you'll be as right as rain in the morning."

*

Dr Derbyshire is a slight, middle-age man with fine yellow-grey hair and blue eyes. He reminds her of one of the characters in her old Happy Families pack of cards – probably owing to his large disproportionate head. Was it Dr Dose or one of the Snips? Her sense of recall seems to have dimmed with time or illness or both. At least, that is why one usually sees doctors – for illness.

Dr. Derbyshire speaks in mellow, sympathetic tones which should be conducive to unburdening herself but isn't. Every time she sees him she finds herself still playing the same old games of self-defence. Too scared to say she's scared. Too confused to say she's confused. But he's a psychiatrist, damn it, it's his job to mind-read and break through barriers. Why make it easy for him? He must do something to earn his whack.

But each time she sees him she's dogged by guilt. She feels she's misusing his valuable time and he's such a busy man, spread too thinly as it is. People on the cusp of illness and health, like herself, should be considerate and spare him the time to get on with the exclusive treatment of bona fide crackpots as he was trained to do.

Or is she mad?

One day he decides to break it to her gently. Talks to her about the outcome of assessments they have been doing since she has been in hospital. He has talked to her about the diagnosis. He has talked to her about treatment and medication and prognosis and what they both can expect in the coming years. He is beating about the bush and talking in euphemisms. Do you understand what I've told you? Do you have any questions?

She hears the word clearly this time. She might have heard it before, here, in the hospital, in relation to herself, but she wasn't listening properly. But she is listening now. Schizophrenia. The beautiful name that sounds more like a pretty foreign female than a horrific condition. Schizophrenic is the adjective. She is schizophrenic. How wonderful these new fancy words are. These medical euphemisms for insanity. Make it sound Greek and unpronounceable and unspellable and you're in business. You've destigmatized it.

And so every Wednesday afternoon, once she has been discharged as an in-patient, she takes the bus up to the psychiatric outpatients' clinic where she settles down to a long wait in the red plastic chairs. While she waits, each sound is greatly enhanced: the heel as it squeaks over the polished herring-bone floor, the rustle of the magazine as pages are turned, the clock as it jumps forward another fraction, the beat of blood as it's pounded around her head and other heads as they wait and wait. Sometimes she will treat herself to an orange juice from the smiling WRVS ladies who look older than the clinic itself.

As the weeks pass she realizes there is something not quite right as she prepares to test-drive this repaired model. It's a day in late November when, walking round the city – a city already studded with Christmas illuminations – it hits her. The overwhelming feeling is tiredness. Or is it weariness? Whatever it is she doesn't want to walk any more, she wants to sit down, and so she finds a snack bar and voyages past coffee puddles and broken plastic spoons and plastic hatches with their sad and wilting offerings. On she goes to the drink-making machine at the end of the counter where she orders coffee. The machine roars and whizzes and her frothy drink is pushed to her in a perfunctory manner. She pays her money and carries her tray on another trudge through more dubious puddles and bursting carrier bags and squawking chits. There are no free tables. She will have to share with that straw-haired woman with skin as tough as elephant hide. She registers the crack of the woman's cigarette as she sucks in the dark plumes to the – no doubt – even darker chambers inside her. Even when she removes the cigarette, the woman's mouth is perpetually ringed for the next inhalation. Amanda soon realizes that life isn't too rosy between the black clouds for her table-mate who immediately starts pouring her troubles onto her. What the hell am I going to do about our Johnnie? He wants a new bike for Christmas, you know, like all his mates at school have got but me fella was laid off last Friday. We promised him. As if we didn't have enough to worry about with our Bernie getting herself into all kinds of trouble, going on the rob with those scallies off the estate...

On the adjacent table a fat man and his half-grown son gnaw into greasy egg-burgers. Now and then the father, spitting bread sawdust as he does so, issues a warning axe-arm at the boy who dodges back on his chair in grinning defiance. Meanwhile, the lean teenaged assistants pay no attention. They shuffle about with their blue check overalls and mass-produced faces, deigning to wipe a table here or clack a few glasses together there; barely scraping together a smile between them. They are certainly not here to be helpful; they are marking time and thinking about tonight.

Why then, Amanda wonders, does she find herself envying this entire miserable gathering? She thinks it could be that they have something that she hasn't. They seem to have found the formula for everyday living which so far she has failed to crack. But it is more than that. Something is missing, though she's not sure what.

She stands up, unrefreshed, but less weary. She knows what to do – if her mind can find no refuge, no escape from the pressing vulgarity, than perhaps her body will if she takes it to somewhere more conducive, like a historical part of the city perhaps. The stately Bluecoat Chambers, for instance.

Soon she is crossing the cobbled courtyard and passing through the building to the smaller quadrangle behind, leading to the display centre. In days gone by, this would have been a sight to conjure with: this silent place with its old-style gas-lamp shining on cobbles which glisten in imperceptible rain. But what does she feel *now*? What she feels now is what she recalls feeling in the past, what she feels now are only second hand remembered feelings, what she ought to feel but can't any more.

*

Her inner eyes have yielded to her outer pair. The outer eyes record nothing but concrete reality and greyness. The world is like an old tarnished coin, one that is commonplace and worthless. Blackness would be preferable because with blackness you can at least feel a kind of perverse pleasure in the martyrdom, the bitter injustice. With blackness you can look forward to the light, the slow dawn. But her surroundings are inescapable these days. The compromising grey abounds – a sort of washed-out, headache pigment. All the coloured threads of a grand tapestry have been unpicked, leaving only the plain sackcloth. This is the colour of her soul then, after all. Sack.

All is not irrevocable surely - just a case of swilling the Largactil and the rest of her pills down the loo. It's most unlikely that her old world has been wholly burnt away beneath the drug-coating of her brain.

But it's all too much effort. This very moment she is too tired. So very tired. Nothing before or behind, nothing to look forward to. Just drifting into safe inactivity with her clay-brain. And so what? It's not so bad really. She's getting to the stage where she couldn't care less.

FOURTEEN

Rosalind has enlisted Amanda to help arrange the deckchairs in the garden, to do any last minute hoovering, to put fresh Pot pourri in Angie's bedroom. Amanda has done this and more, like the box of coloured tissues she's put on Angie's dressing table, which she said they used to do at the Heathfield Hotel.

Angie and Neville are due to arrive any time from two o'clock onwards, and Rosalind is already feeling a nervous thrill at the thought.

At noon, when the sun is starting to get really hot, she goes indoors to slice and dice and toss and stir a host of salad ingredients. They are as bright and colourful as the sea of dazzling petals outside. Summer hums like a fan across the garden, flies buzz in and out of the open windows and doors, and the sky is white with the fierce heat of the sun. Everything is so warm and still, yet tremulous, like the butterflies and flowers that stir the utopia out there, and she is soon lured back into her deckchair. She squints over at Amanda who sits in the shade stroking Tinker's fully-stretched white tummy. Amanda is now doing several hours of voluntary work each week; she gets hungry in the mornings and evenings and has gained some weight from her medication. Rosalind has herself been drinking considerably less. The odd glass of wine here and there, with meals, in the evening, that sort of thing, but much more under her control. As she closes her eyes she wonders, sleepily, whether Neville and Angie will be suitably impressed by the changes in them both. Whether they will decide to stay longer than a week, or even seriously consider coming home for good...

She wakes to find herself in the shade and Angie bending over her laden with shopping bags, laughing herself silly.

"Wakey wakey! We've brought some goodies with us!" Angie hands the bags to Rosalind.

They kiss. Angie is wearing a white Broderie Anglaise dress and sunglasses, her hair tied up in a way not unlike Rosalind's. She could almost be her natural daughter; people used to think so. Neville too looks sun-browned and healthy. She tells him as much as they hold one another tightly.

"You too, Rosalind."

"I've missed you a lot, Neville."

"Me too."

"I bet you say that to all your women, doesn't he, Angie?"

"What other women? I've had no time for that! Been busy working hard and establishing my business." He looks over at Amanda. "You're looking really well, Amanda! Come and give us a hug then."

"She's going away again soon to work at that hotel in Devon," says Rosalind. "Aren't you, Amanda?"

"Yes. They're taking on more staff for the busiest months – July to September."

"That's marvellous," says Neville. "Great news."

They catch up on news over lunch: Angie's new boyfriend Charles, Angie's journalism course. It hadn't even occurred to Rosalind that Angie would have found herself a new life in London; that she would have changed so noticeably. But there's something quite different about her, something that you wouldn't have picked up from her letters alone. She's more sensible and mature, rather more aloof. It's almost as though Amanda – that is Amanda as she was – were sitting there displaying that characteristic caginess and reticence. Rosalind finds it bothers her slightly; it makes her think that perhaps Angie won't like the food or the house or the road any more, or this narrow-minded suburb. She fears she will appear dull and untravelled in comparison.

Later, upstairs, she is reassured to see more of the Angie of old, talking and laughing with Amanda. That's a sight of long ago, certainly. Angie is saying, "We'll go shopping next week, Amanda, and deck you out with a new wardrobe. You can't hit the social scene in Devon with those old clothes now, can you? And what about a different hairstyle?"

Rosalind comes in and stands behind Amanda protectively, one hand on the shoulder of her lilac blouse. At the moment her hair is tied back in a way which suits Amanda – it is both simple and effective. "Amanda's all right as she is, aren't you, Amanda?"

"But I wanted to spend some of my hard-earned dosh," says Angie. "Well, Charlie's anyway. I saw this lovely red dress in Bold Street earlier. I mean how many times in your life has someone offered to buy you something from a shop in Bold Street?"

"It's not Amanda's style," says Rosalind. "Is it, Amanda?"

In an instant, Rosalind prefers Amanda to the way Angie is now. She has never experienced this so acutely. Before it was something she knew she ought to feel, though she was never quite convinced by her feelings, whereas now it is categorical. Amanda is like a priceless piece of mended porcelain, a piece never fully appreciated until it got broken. But Rosalind treasures it all the more, especially as she alone knows the hard work involved in sticking it back together. If she is completely honest she resents Angie fiddling and interfering in things she hasn't got a clue about.

*

A week later Billy taps Amanda on the shoulder as she comes out of Selfridges with a couple of small bags.

"Fancy bumping into you here," he says. "I thought Rosalind said you'd gone away to Devon."

"I go next week," she says. "I was just buying myself some new things. Some earrings and these ankle socks."

"Well I'm glad I caught you before you went. I didn't want you just sneaking off without saying goodbye."

"As if."

"I'm on my lunch break so I haven't got a lot of time," he says, "but I often like to walk down towards Pier Head. Maybe we could call in for a swift half if we see anywhere we fancy on the way. What d'you reckon?"

"Fine by me."

As they walk in the breezy city sunshine, his tie blowing over his shoulder like all the other white-collar males in the windy city, Billy thinks back to that first time he walked through town with Amanda, that evening when Angie had left him in the lurch with that spare ticket for *Cabaret*. He thinks how different Amanda is to then, how more self-assured.

He spots a pub which, in contrast to the brightness outside, looks dark and cool. A large airy pub with big fans turning on the ceiling, and beer straight from the wood, a pool table, and a hulky old jukebox.

Amanda insists on getting the first beer in and so Billy sits and flips his beer mat while he waits.

"Ta very much, Amanda. It's not often a lady buys me a bevvy."

"Should I put something on the juke box?"

"I wouldn't waste your money. I've been here before

and it can take yonks to hear your records." He sups his pint and wipes beer froth from his lip. "You know I met up with Angie for a drink last Friday. Did she tell you?"

"Yes, she did."

"I'm forgiven, you know, for…" The unspoken hangs large in the air between them. "It's all water under the bridge anyway, now that she's copped off with some Cockney fella. Did she go back to London on Sunday?"

"Yes. She and Neville."

"What does Rosalind think about that then? I mean she's going to be a bit lonely what with you off next week an' all."

"Oh I don't think she minds that much," says Amanda. "She feels really positive about Neville's visit and they talked about her possibly moving to London. Nothing definite, but she may go down to visit and take it from there."

As she talks, Billy sees her 'recovered' self as almost too good to be true. She's doing a splendid job of pretending to be normal with her trained smiles and rehearsed phrases and appropriate replies but she is too normal when you consider how strange she has been. She is trying to be what she isn't and it grates. Just like it did with Angie when she tried to pass those poems off as her own. Even so, he finds himself saying, "I'm really made up for you, with your new job and that."

"Old job don't you mean."

"Oh yeah," he says. "Anyway maybe you'll be able to write some more of your poetry in your free afternoons."

She shakes her head and pulls a face as if to dissociate herself from such mad doings.

"Why not?" he says. "You've got a talent there. Don't waste it."

"No." She shakes her head more dismissively this time. "That was then. Part of *that* time. I want to forget all that and move forward."

*

The following week, Amanda heads off to Devon as planned. She finds there have been a few noticeable changes at the Heathfield, not least of which is the extra star rating. It now boasts four stars with new standards to match. For instance, the staff all have new uniforms and titles. There are no chambermaids or waitresses any more but housekeeping assistants and restaurant assistants. Amanda supposes that the upgraded uniform was introduced to reflect the extra star. Before, they wore brown and white candy-striped overalls with plain brown aprons she recalls. Now the overall is a dark brown with a brown and white flowery apron. Not only this but the linen reflects this smart brown theme: that is, one dark brown sheet and one cream one per bed, one dark brown pillow case for the under pillows and one cream one for the top pillows. In the bathrooms too, the same contrasting colour coordination is applied.

Most of the old faces aren't there either, except Glynis the housekeeper, who has put on even more weight, and Maude, the mature non-resident room maid who left shortly after Amanda arrived last time, and Taff the gormless waiter who appears somewhat less childish than she remembers. There is no Dee this year – she has gone to work on the Isle of Wight – while the others, Val and Linda, who were both here again last year apparently, have each gone further afield to work this year. In Europe, it is said.

Rather than the chalets, most of the female members are now accommodated in the main part of the hotel - in the least attractive rooms with views of the metal fire escape and the like. Amanda has been allocated a room with a shy nineteen-year-old called Sharon.

"I'm a student," said Sharon, on her first meeting with

Amanda. "I'm studying French at Bristol. I've never done anything like this before. Have you?"

"Yes. I was here two years ago."

"Oh everyone seems to be more experienced than me," said Sharon. "I feel so naïve."

Amanda soon finds herself taking Sharon in hand, showing her all the short cuts and tricks of the trade. This is a new role for Amanda. It has come on her by default. Sharon is indeed naïve and sweet and all smiles, and Amanda sees herself as that bit older and wiser.

They make a good team, she and Sharon, working the Hacienda between them. If one of them is feeling off colour one day, for whatever reason, the other will offer to do some of her rooms.

It is in this atmosphere of goodwill that Amanda decides to tell Sharon a secret a two. They are polishing the solid dark wood on the second floor landing in the oldest part of the hotel when Amanda says, "I must get some water so I can take my pills."

Polite as ever, Sharon has never dared ask about these pills, so Amanda, seizing the moment, decides to put her out of her misery. "I had a nervous breakdown last summer...these keep me stable."

"Really?" says Sharon with that look of surprise of hers. "I sometimes think I might have one. I started to feel very stressed at uni last year. Fortunately my brother is there too. He's a lot more confident than me and helps me."

"Is he older than you?"

"No, we're twins," she says.

"Oh I see," says Amanda, impressed by her own sense of calmness at this revelation. "Do you like being a twin?"

"Well yes," says Sharon. "I suppose we're not like other twins, being fraternal, and boy and girl. But it's like there's another part of you in a different body. It's hard to explain to other people..."

Amanda nods knowingly. All that twin stuff, all that business with Jo, it was all delusion, all part of the illness, she understands that now. She is simply a singleton whose sickness gave her a rare insight into twin life.

*

Back in Blundellsands, Rosalind puts in the tortoiseshell stud earrings Neville once bought her and slips on her smart black shoes. She has a funny feeling about today. She wonders what Amanda is doing this very minute and makes a firm resolve to go and visit her in Devon as she promised, perhaps combining it with a detour to London so that she can call in on Neville. She's not sure of her future with Neville but they need to take things a step at a time at this stage.

Life without great tides of alcohol has certainly tuned-up her mind and she has been able to go further back through those misty lands marked Rodney and beyond. It begins each time with that mental photograph album in her head because it would be too much trouble trying to locate the real photographs, somewhere at the bottom of the many boxes stowed behind the rowing machine in the spare room. Anyway, the ones inside her head are just as good because sometimes they don't stay fixed, sometimes the people and places move along. First there will be Neville in his many focussed poses, and then Southport with its past-its-best opulence, its facade of gentility, and then some of the pictures start to fade or they are few and far between, as with jolly-faced Joe. There is still only one of Love Child Joe – huge, gold-bordered and unerasable. And then there is Rodney. Lately it is Rodney who has been coming to life in small chunks of cine film, rather than still pictures. But it is *that* particular one she has never dared to watch in its entirety again until recently. The one where she has just left Rodney for Joe. She's fought hard to keep it away, but now there's no stopping her mental projectionist, and she sees Rodney all forlorn and devoid of his family.

Then he is gone and she is sitting in the park with her pram, plots of cultivated flowers all around. There is no sun, in fact it's quite dark and cloudy which makes the flowers seem altogether brighter. Joe has been wonderful but from Rodney there has been no word. Rodney is a civilized man but his silence is beginning to frighten her...

It looks like it may rain so she gets up and pushes her pram along the road towards the Co-op where she has a few things to buy. She parks the pram outside and as she goes into the store she feels she's being watched. It makes her feel slightly uncomfortable for a moment or two but then she turns her attention to her shopping list.

It's not until she comes out of the store that her face turns white. One of the twins has disappeared. Louise. Yes, it is Louise because the one with her crown on the right side of her head – that is, Rosalind's right and Louise's left – is still in the pram asleep. That's the only certain way of telling which one is which when they are apart. When you think about it, twins, being two halves of the same egg, are mirror images of one another. They are each other in reverse.

Amanda wakes up and cries. The pram must feel cold and empty. She has noticed something missing. Rosalind tucks her in and then she sees Rodney, standing by his car. Louise is inside, in a carrycot on the back seat. Rodney is crying. "Please," he says. "Just let me keep one of them. Let me keep Louise. She's all I have left." She knows he can make it difficult for her if he wants, he's a lawyer after all, there's a firm of top-notch solicitors who might lose her both of the twins if he so decreed. "I will give you a divorce. I will withdraw from your life and let you get on with it in peace. Just let me have one of my daughters." It would have sounded insane coming from anyone else but Rodney is very persuasive. "I promise to look after her. I will pay for the best nanny. Please, let's just have a trial period. How about three months?" Rosalind is weeping now. She feels sorry for him, he shouldn't be made to suffer, he shouldn't have to lose everything. It's a way of paying off her guilt.

"Three months then, Rodney," she says. "And if it doesn't work out on either side... "

He lifts his head towards the sky, his hands in the prayer position. "Thank you, God," he says, his eyes closing briefly.

"Look after her for me, Rodney," she says, and then cries all the way home.

Of course, that had to be it after the first three months.

Rosalind puts on her bracelet, the one that matches the tortoiseshell earrings. She had to make a clean break, otherwise it would have become too painful, so that's what they did, severing all links, all reminders, everyone played by the rules, even jolly Joe.

But here in Atherton House, she has this wrong feeling about today. You just know. She feels terribly subdued as she goes to collect the post. She bends down to the pile of letters on the mat but the one that confirms her deep sense of unease is the one with the Cornwall postmark. She knows what is inside, even before opening it...

*

Her mother arrived at the Heathfield half an hour ago where she has booked in to stay the night, on her way back from Cornwall. She has been given Room 25 in the old part of the hotel, with back views of the hotel terrace-gardens, but incorporating a chunk of sea out of the side window.

"My, my!" Rosalind said when she first saw the hotel and her room. "Isn't this grand? Why aren't you in uniform?"

"I'm off duty," said Amanda. "Strictly speaking, I'm not supposed to frequent the guest areas when I've finished work."

"Oh but this is an exception," said Rosalind. "I'm your mother, after all. I'm sure you're allowed to join me for a drink in the bar later."

"I daresay. This once."

"Well I must just go to the bathroom to freshen up. It's so nice to have a bathroom en suite. Did you do this room?"

"No. Maude does this floor."

"Well she's done a very thorough job, I must say. I'll have to give her a good tip," she said, clicking on the bathroom light. "Now I won't be long. Perhaps you could make us both a nice cup of tea."

Amanda now hears the running of water and flicks on the television, though there's little on that interests her. "Mum," she calls, as she puts the kettle on, "why did you go to Cornwall again? To see friends did you say?"

There's no answer. Her mother obviously didn't hear. She will have to ask her again when she comes out. But Rosalind doesn't appear for ages until eventually Amanda knocks on the bathroom door and says, "Mum? Have you fallen asleep in there? I made you some tea ages ago." She thinks she hears faint snuffles and when her mother does emerge, it's clear there have indeed been tears. Not just a few tears either.

"What's the matter mum?"

"It's nothing," she says as she unzips her case and fishes out a new packet of tissues. Amanda just catches sight of black clothes and a black hat, a colour which, on

137

Rosalind, can only mean one thing.

"You've been to a funeral, haven't you? That's why you went to Cornwall, isn't it?"

"I'm sorry," says Rosalind, unable to control the upsurge of new tears. "I didn't want to spoil our time together."

"I thought you came down here especially to see me but you had to come down this way anyway."

"I'm sorry," says Rosalind again. Amanda hands her the box of pink tissues from the dressing table and Rosalind tugs out a few sheets. "Thank you. They think of everything here, don't they?"

"Whose was it anyway?"

"No one you knew." Rosalind wipes her nose with the whole clump of tissues. "It was just an old school friend who was very dear to me."

"I've never heard you mention *any* school friends. What was her name?"

"Louise. Her name was Louise. Please don't question me any more," she says. "I've had an exhausting couple of days and now I just want to relax."

"I'm sorry, I should have been more sensitive." Amanda suddenly feels guilty. "I'll tell you what, why don't we go down and have that drink in the bar? I'm sure a stiff drink will work wonders."

"I can't go down looking like this. Not with my eyes all puffy and everything."

"Just splash a bit of water on your eyes. No one will notice. The lights are all low down there."

Dazed, Rosalind does as Amanda tells her. "How do I look now?"

"Fine."

"Are you coming down then?"

"In five minutes," says Amanda. "I just need to finish my tea and go to the loo."

"I'll wait for you then."

"No, you go on down. I won't be long."

Once Rosalind has gone, Amanda has a quick mad rummage through Rosalind's case. She digs deep, way beneath the black garments, for something, she doesn't know what. But there is nothing. No bit of paper with a scribbled down address, no documents at all. Oh silly me, she thinks as she tidies up the case. They will be in Rosalind's handbag of course.

Down in the bar, Amanda sees that apart from her mother there is only one other guest, a middle-aged man, who seems to be carrying on a one-sided conversation with Rosalind across several tables. Amanda immediately goes to her mother's rescue.

"I'm so glad you came in when you did, Amanda. I don't think he's taken the hint."

"Oh you must be the daughter," the man says. "Mind if I join you?"

Amanda turns her back to the man and whispers to her mother. "We don't have to stay down here. We could always order some drinks at the bar and take them upstairs."

"You're a genius," says Rosalind, getting to her feet. "I was beginning to feel so conspicuous here."

"You two abandoning me?" calls the man, as they slip away together.

Once upstairs, Amanda's next task is to separate her mother from her handbag. The only possible way is when her mother goes in the bathroom which won't give her ample time really but it's her only option unless Rosalind were to have a bath. She supposes she could send Rosalind down for some more drinks but Rosalind is sure to take her handbag with her, rather than just her purse.

"Did you say you wanted to go out for a meal tonight mum? Or do you want to eat at the hotel?"

139

"To be honest, I'm not that hungry," says Rosalind. "Maybe we can get something later unless you're hungry now. I've got some biscuits somewhere."

"No I'm not that hungry at the moment either," says Amanda, seeing an opportunity opening up. "Why don't you have a long hot bath, mum? It might make you feel better."

"Oh I don't know. "

"You may as well make the most of the en suite bathroom while you've got it."

"I suppose I could be really decadent and take my Martini in with me."

Amanda smiles, ostensibly at her mother, but really to herself. Her mother will be in the bath for at least twenty minutes, which is time enough. She waits until she hears the plop of feet climbing into the bath...

Quickly she makes a bee-line for the handbag, opens it, and is bombarded by the sheer volume of items: make-up, address book, hair brush, Paracetamol, perfume, cheque book. Most of this she can ignore, she thinks as she scrabbles her way to the wrinkled wad of papers: postcards, letters, an old prescription, medical card, receipts. Feverishly she scours the letters: one from Neville, a recent one from herself, a postcard from Angie, a silver wedding invitation from one of the neighbours, and other official things.

Through her panic she has moments of complete lucidity and thinks to undo the zip of the hidden compartment in the handbag. And right there, solitary and fairly pristine, is the thing she's been looking for, the letter postmarked Cornwall. She opens it out and sees that it is signed from Rodney. Her hands tremble as she tries to read it all at once. But it is a blur to her, she is shaking uncontrollably now as her eyes alight on key phrases and names and words. *It's sad sad news I'm afraid, Louise killed in a car crash, funeral on Tuesday, feel so wretched, never have taken her, would still be here today, you would still have both twins...*

And then Rosalind emerges from the bathroom too soon, something about the water not being hot enough or something.

FIFTEEN

As she leaves Bodmin Parkway station, Rosalind sees Rodney waiting against his car, dressed in an unseasonal pale coat. He approaches her, kisses her on the cheek, and then puts her case in the boot, before driving her back to his modest little mews house in Padstow.

"Ah good," he says as he opens a door straight into the living room. "Judith has prepared the fire. She is my housekeeper by the way," he says. "Please, come in from the cold and make yourself at home. I expect you'd like a hot drink."

"A coffee would be super."

Rosalind sweeps her eyes around the room. Such a small room but it has everything: dark tasteful furniture, the open fire, watercolours by various Cornish artists. Funny then, that she should be the one to end up alone in a three-storey house. It is far too big for one – she will have to make a decision on it soon, when other things have been sorted out.

It's been nearly three months since Louise's funeral. She and Rodney promised they would keep in touch afterwards; they both had so many questions for each other. He wanted to know all about Amanda, to meet her, and of course when this was suggested Amanda was healthy, better than she'd been for many years, and so he knows nothing about the schizophrenia. Rosalind in turn wanted to know all about the real Louise, rather than the embellished version one tends to get at funerals.

Rodney brings in the coffees and as he lights the fire he says, "Well, what do you think of my humble abode then?"

"It's lovely."

"Well it's adequate for me and...it was adequate for…" He starts to choke on his words. "I say, would you like a brandy or something? Judith has prepared a lovely casserole which we can have soon. I'll just put it in the oven."

"Rodney?" Rosalind follows him into the kitchen. "Remind me, how many years you've lived here."

"Ten years," he says. "Before that we lived in that much bigger town house in Truro…I'm sorry, I'll be fine in a moment, Rosalind. Now, dinner's in the oven, table's laid ... "

"It looks beautiful, the table."

"Ah good. That was my contribution. I do love silver and candles. Eating should be a tactile experience, don't you think?"

"The azaleas give it that extra touch too," says Rosalind. "Especially at this time of year."

Once the meal gets underway and their minds lubricated with several glasses of wine, Rosalind unleashes her interim life in disjointed bursts: baby Joe, Neville, Angie.

"So you lost another child?" says Rodney. "How terrible for you."

"It was. But your loss must be greater at the moment…being so recent."

"I'm sorry we lost contact after the first few years but I knew that's what you wanted. I always tried to respect your wishes."

"After losing little Joe I just had to shut off the pain. The whole past. Do you understand?"

"Perfectly. I've never really forgiven myself for persuading you to part with Louise. Several times, during the early years, I would start out on the journey north, planning to return her to you, but I could never quite do it."

"It's all so long ago now. What's done is done."

"I suppose so," he says. "But I often wonder what she'd have been like if she'd been brought up on Merseyside. She knew she was born there obviously but she always said she would have hated Liverpool." He rests his cutlery while he sups more wine. "It conjured up for her black buildings and dirty docks and shifty people with a humour she could never quite grasp."

"So what did you tell her about her mother?"

"Forgive me," he says, his pale eyes looking straight across at her, "but I said that you just couldn't cope with motherhood. That one day you'd just vanished and the last I'd heard you'd gone to live in Australia."

"And she believed you?"

"She had no reason not to. She asked a few questions, you know, during mid-childhood, but she seemed to accept the 'official line' with no major doubts or traumas as far as I could see."

"And did she know of Amanda's existence?"

"I told her that she had a twin sister who'd died in childbirth," he says, "which sort of added to the authenticity of her disappearing mother. Does that sound terrible? I suppose that was why I never did make it to Liverpool because I'd have had to explain the mysterious appearance of her twin sister." He takes his last mouthful and closes his knife and fork. "And what did you tell Amanda?"

"Worse. I told her you were dead and I never let on that she was a twin but she seemed to know anyway."

"Really? How extraordinary. In what way?"

"She occasionally mentioned her twin. That's all. But please, tell me more about Louise."

"I still can't believe she's gone. Another young girl with a bright future – gone, snuffed out in her prime." He reaches for the wine and refills their glasses. "There's something dreadfully impersonal and random about car accidents," he says, "whereas murder, albeit foul, is at least personal, planned, meant-to-be. Does that sound a terrible thing to say?"

"No, not if it's the way you feel," she says, suddenly aware at this late stage that she's just not hungry. The last few mouthfuls of casserole have been hard work, eaten out of politeness, but now she really can't eat any more, though Rodney doesn't seem to have noticed. "So how about telling me more about Louise," she says. "What was she like as a person? You don't mind me asking you, do you?"

"No." He shines an unused knife on the tablecloth. "No, of course not. I want to talk about her. It's all I have left to keep her memory alive." He dabs the corner of his mouth with the fawn serviette, and offers Rosalind fruit or cheese and biscuits but she is full up she says. "In that case," he says, as he unwraps a cigar, "do you mind awfully if I…?"

"You go ahead. I'll join you with a cigarette."

"I know it's terribly clichéd, but Louise was one of these people who had everything – looks, brains, success." He goes to the sideboard. "Here's a photograph of her," he says, handing it to Rosalind. "That was taken at her graduation."

The scrolled frame feels cold as she holds it between her hands. Here is the other side of Amanda, the happy, confident, achieving side that has barely seen the light of day. Her eyes are filling up but she's smiling. "Just a normal young woman," she says.

145

"Normal, yes." He holds his head back, and thinks for a moment, his cigar up by his temples. "Though I often wondered whether not knowing her mother had affected her."

"And had it in your opinion?"

"No not unduly." He passes her an ashtray which looks vaguely familiar. He did used to smoke very occasionally in the old days, she'd forgotten. "Or maybe that's just me trying to convince myself. If I'm truly honest it must have. It would affect any child – wouldn't it? – being parted from her mother." He coughs, and snuffs out his cigar. "But she always seemed so well-adjusted and she had a very good nanny during her early years. I made sure of that."

"So she wasn't odd in any way?"

"Odd? No. That's an 'odd' thing to say." He picks a grape from the fruit bowl. "Why do you ask that?"

"Well, it's just that Amanda is."

"Is– ?"

"Special."

"A genius?"

"Not normal," she says. "You know – gaga. Bats in the belfry. Schizo. Whatever you want to call it."

Rodney gives an instinctive laugh, he doesn't quite know what other emotion to display. "Of all the things I'd bargained for," he says, "this wasn't one of them. So I was right first time. A genius!"

"I'm being serious, Rodney."

"Great wits are sure to madness close allied…who was it that wrote that? It seems to have slipped my mind temporarily."

"Rodney, please…"

"I've lost one daughter and the other is mad," he laughs ironically. "I suppose some people have worse. Some people have no children at all!"

"That isn't all," she says.

"You mean there's something else?"

"She's in hospital right at this moment. In Exeter. She's been there for two months and I still haven't been to see her."

"Good grief, Rosalind. You really know how to drop a bombshell!" He picks up the cigar again, though it stays unlit. "It makes complete sense now why you were being so reticent about her. Well...I don't know what I'm supposed to say."

"The thing is," she says, calmer now that she's spilled the worst, "the reason I want to stay here for a few days is that I'm going to visit her tomorrow. I've just ignored most of the letters from the hospital up until now because I just couldn't cope."

"I quite understand."

"I'm not expecting you to come to the hospital with me or anything like that yet," she says. "In fact it's probably better that I go alone. But she saw your letter Rodney. The one you wrote to me about Louise's accident, and it tipped her over the edge again."

SIXTEEN

Lines of rain slant towards the boggy ground as Rosalind stands outside the hospital – a grim red-bricked place, not unlike she had anticipated. If she is going to turn back then she better do it now, she thinks, while she still has the chance. But something compels her onwards through the main entrance. There are arrows pointing to departments of every description: neurological, orthopaedic, X-ray, physiotherapy, geriatric. She is almost holding her breath through the rabbit warren of medical-smelling corridors until, at last, she sees an arrow to the psychiatric wing. It is predictably tucked away at the back, away from the main hub. When she reaches the wing she retreats into the toilets to compose herself.

With renewed resolve, she steps out and accosts a passing nurse. "Excuse me, I've come to visit a relative on the female ward...could you -?"

"Follow me," says the young nurse, walking confidently through the doors to the ward. Though obviously busy, the nurse is obliging and deposits Rosalind in the small office on the ward. "This lady has come to visit a relative," she announces to an older-looking nurse with yellow stick-teeth, before hurrying off.

The older nurse looks at Rosalind sternly. "Which one?"

"I spoke to the ward clerk this morning about visiting

my daughter."

"Mrs Court, I presume."

"I'm Mrs Court, that's right."

"I see," the nurse says, brusquely. "Well I don't expect it'll do much good."

"I'm sorry?"

"Miss Court's had no visitors, you know. Not since that nice student friend of hers had to go back to university. The patients who do best are the ones who get the visits. The ones whose families work with us. Patients shouldn't be here long-term."

"I live in Liverpool," says Rosalind, in her defence. "I got down here as soon as I could."

"Come this way, please."

Rosalind knows she has got off to a bad start with this nurse. She follows her onto the ward, apologetically at first and then with growing defiance. What can this horrid woman know about family life anyway? She looks the product of orphanages and other grim institutions and Rosalind finds herself despising the back view of the smoke-brown bun drooping down the neck, like a symbol of toppled power. She hears the nurse muttering as she walks, "…a complete waste of time." Rosalind stays silent. There's little point in coming to blows with this dreadful nurse who's probably a bit unhinged herself - it's probably an occupational hazard.

Rosalind looks around her. The ward is clean enough, though it's also impersonal and old-fashioned. She sees that only three beds on the ward are occupied. On her immediate right a woman, aged about fifty, has just started to recite limericks at the top of her voice. THERE WAS A YOUNG LADY FROM CREWE, WHO FILLED HER VAGINA WITH -

"OK OK, I think we've heard quite enough of that one, Betty," says the Horrid Nurse while Rosalind winces at what poor Amanda must have to endure, cooped up with this lot. "Anyway, I thought you said you weren't feeling well. You sound well enough to get up if you ask me." Betty pouts and launches into a new limerick. THERE WAS A YOUNG LADY FROM EALING -

Opposite Betty, on the left side of the ward, a girl in her twenties lies asleep with a plaster-cast ruff immuring her neck. (Rosalind decides that she must be heavily sedated to be able to sleep at all through the jolly foghorn voice of Betty.) Further down on the left is another patient but there is no sign of Amanda – just one or two nurses milling around.

The Horrid Nurse walks on, past the sleeping invalid. Rosalind feels a fresh wave of motivation: to get Amanda out of here as soon as possible. In a way, the Horrid Nurse is right. This is no place to remain. The Horrid Nurse is still moving steadily through the deserted ward. The rest of the patients must be in the Day Room. Amanda must be there too, watching television or playing cards or doing some crocheting, or perhaps she is having some Group Therapy. These are the sort of things they do in places like this, don't they?

The Horrid Nurse slows down. She is approaching the third patient on the ward now who is clearly not Amanda. Evidently the nurse has to deal with this pixie-faced adolescent because she is stopping. Rosalind lingers a few yards behind and sighs anxiously. This woman is taking a special, almost sadistic, delight in procrastination it would seem.

"Miss Court. A visitor for you." The Horrid Nurse taps the foot of the pixie's bed with her slender nicotine fingers. Then she is gone.

Yes it is! Hell – she can see it now! Amanda is half-sitting in bed wearing a white gown, the pillows stacked behind her on the headboard. Her hair, fluffed in brittle wisps, looks as though it has been subjected to the loppings of some amateur. But it is the eyes which get to her most. Vacant and shadowed purple.

"Amanda," says Rosalind tentatively. "Amanda, it's me. Your mother."

But Amanda isn't even looking or responding. Rosalind sits down on the bed. "I've brought some magazines for you…"

She feels ill at ease, her warmth strained and misleading, like winter sun through a window, and her voice inharmonious, like a growler in a school choir. "I'll get you out of here, Amanda. I promise."

After a while of this, Rosalind, bolder now, goes in search of the Horrid Nurse. "Why isn't my daughter answering me?" she asks. "Or even acknowledging me?"

"The psychiatrist is here if you wish to speak with him."

"Yes I do."

She expects to wait, but almost immediately a man introducing himself as Dr. Savage asks her into his office.

"So you are Amanda's mother," he says, looking not at her, but at the file on his desk.

"That's right," she says, with deference. "I've tried speaking to her but she doesn't seem to recognize me."

"I'm afraid Amanda's condition has deteriorated since she was admitted back in September." His tone sounds human at least.

"Isn't there anything you can do?"

"With all due respects, Mrs Court, I think in this case you are the one in a position to do something. It cannot be over-stated, the importance of family support…" So he's in on it too, the guilt-laying. "Our records show that we contacted you, her next of kin, on several occasions but it was met with no response."

"I'm sorry…I've had a lot to deal with myself these

last few months." She realizes how lame it must sound.

"I'm not trying to apportion blame," he says, suddenly aware, perhaps, of coming across too heavy-handed. "I'm glad that you've come now because I think regular visits from you may be the very thing that's needed."

"I'm staying with her father. Rodney Court. I'm hoping to persuade him to visit her."

"All the better," says Dr Savage, and then his phone rings. "Do excuse me…"

*

That evening, Rosalind tells Rodney everything. About the nasty nurse and Betty the jolly nutcase and the shock of seeing Amanda looking so awful. She is exhausted but Rodney sends her upstairs for a relaxing hot bath and by the time she emerges again she is suitably revived. Not only that but Rodney has given Judith the night off and prepared a superb fish dish for their supper tonight. Again, out come the candles, and the flowers, the best silver.

Rodney has that charming glint in his eye as he pours more wine. "Do you know, Rosalind," he says "I could cook like this for you all the time."

She laughs. "And where would that leave Judith?"

"Do you like housework?"

"No, not particularly."

"There you are then."

"This sauce is wonderful, Rodney," she says, pleased that she has more of an appetite tonight.

"I'm glad you like it," he says. "But don't change the subject. Maybe I should say it again more emphatically. Rosalind, why don't you come and live here with me?"

She smiles again, not sure how to reply.

"I'm not sure how to take your silence," he says, raising his glass. "Do I take it that you're giving it some serious thought?"

"There's just so much to think about," she says. "There's Amanda, and then there's Neville to consider and the house..."

"I apologize. I don't mean to put pressure on you. Well, yes I do. But I just wanted you to know how I feel. How I've always felt. For me, there's never been anyone else. "

"What never?"

"Rodney and Rosalind. I've always thought how well our names go together. They belong together."

"Rodney?" she says, as he chinks his glass against hers. "Will you come and see Amanda?"

"I'll do anything if you say you'll move in with me," he says, as she pictures a sunny scene: Rodney's mews house in the summer with pots of geraniums in the passage and the slatted shadows of a garden bench, Tinker at their legs.

"Can I get you some dessert?" he says, clearing away the dinner plates. He opens the fridge and returns to the table bearing a glass of lemon sorbet in each hand. "Seriously," he says, as they pick up their spoons in unison. "I'm not sure about visiting Amanda yet. I need more time."

"More time," she repeats, as the sorbet melts on her tongue. "Yes. That's just what I need too. More time to think about my future."

"Of course," he agrees. "But please say you'll give it your careful consideration. That's all I ask."

"Oh I will," she says. "I will."

*

Rosalind returns to the hospital the following day. She is in a more positive frame of mind. She knows what to expect today. She is also feeling uplifted by the attention Rodney has been paying her – something quite unexpected among all the recent doom and gloom.

There is, thank goodness, a different nurse today, one with an Asian accent – an altogether friendlier species than yesterday's – who Rosalind approaches without hesitation because some things have been bothering her.

"Does she feed herself?" she asks.

"Sometimes," says today's nurse. "Most of the time she is compliant. Other times she needs the encouragement."

"And what about washing and dressing and going to the toilet?"

"The same thing really," says the nurse. "Sometimes she will do these things after the first request, other times she has to be coaxed."

"So she does get out of bed sometimes."

"Oh yes," says the nurse. "It's just these last two weeks she's been a bit poorly. They get prone to infection, you see."

"And does she speak to anyone at all?"

The young nurse smiles as though sifting through a checklist of acceptable replies. "Not so much," she says. "It's the medication," she adds diplomatically. "It can prevent some of them from joining in with activities. But Dr Savage thinks you can help her."

"I'd like to know how."

"Just by coming and talking to her. I see you've brought some flowers with you. Let me get something to put them in."

"Well I thought she might like something bright and cheery to look at," says Rosalind.

The nurse returns with a plastic vase, a few inches of water in the bottom. Rosalind supposes they're not allowed glass jars in case the patients slash their wrists or someone else's.

She sees that the rest of the ward is completely empty today apart from Amanda – no Betty with her lewd limericks, no neck-ruff woman. At least she won't have to put up with an off-putting audience, she thinks, as she prepares herself for another monologue with Amanda.

"Look, Amanda, I've brought you some flowers."

But again, like yesterday, no matter what she says, there is no response.

*

Tuesday and Wednesday each follow a similar pattern. Amanda really does look under the weather, as though thought and conversation are too much to bear. Once or twice, she glances blankly in Rosalind's direction before looking away again at nothing in particular. Once or twice she wanders out of bed, and is immediately taken in hand. There's always someone there, accompanying her to the toilet; supervising her every move.

On Thursday there is another patient occupying the bed next to Amanda. She is what you might call volatile, a bit of a yarn-spinner. Emma is her name and Emma boasts about how she is going home soon although Rosalind senses she will probably be here for a while yet. Still, she likes Emma; she is someone to talk to, someone young and intelligent, even if a bit nutty. In fact Emma talks constantly, Rosalind has noticed, even if it's mostly at, rather than with, others.

Emma arches over sideways to comb through her beautiful hair which is luscious and honey-coloured, weeping down her nightdress like a willow tree, and it has Rosalind wondering how it is that Emma has been allowed to keep her hair while Amanda's has been hacked short. Emma reaches for her gold-etched compact mirror on top of her side-table and crayons her lips damson. She then hides the lipstick under her pillow. She looks like she might be the highly-strung daughter of a doctor or vicar or something, perhaps a suicide attempt, thinks

Rosalind, searching Emma's wrists for a giveaway stitch or scar or bandage but there are none.

"I'm poorly today," says Emma. "Normally I'd be supervising the lupins."

"Lupins?"

"You know – the *loo*-nies."

Rosalind smiles.

"Do you want to hear a joke?" asks Emma. "Well not a joke exactly but something I made up once. It goes like this. Neurotics build castles in the air, psychotics live in them, and the psychiatrist charges the rent. Funny, isn't it?"

Rosalind senses a vague air of familiarity about it, certain that it isn't Emma's own invention but it wouldn't do good to say so. Instead she smiles. Emma has a zingy optimism about her even if it is wholly inappropriate and anyway she's a suitable neighbour for Amanda. Someone has placed them together thoughtfully, like guests at a dinner party, although so far all this effervescing talk has washed right over Amanda.

*

Friday is a dismal day, weatherwise, but for Rosalind's sake, Rodney has agreed to come with her to the hospital. The sky may look bleak, hanging low, pregnant with rain, but thankfully the air is very mild. Splintered conkers crack beneath their tread, and they have to keep their eyes perpetually on the ground as they pick their way through what could be mushy leaves or something dubious left by a dog.

Standing outside the grim hospital, Rodney has mixed feelings about coming here today. In one sense he's glad that Amanda is a completely different kettle of fish than Louise – it would greatly disturb him to be confronted with an echo of Louise, wouldn't it? Or perhaps it would console him.

Just outside the ward itself, they see a howling purple-faced woman being physically restrained by three members of staff in the corridor. The noise is harrowing, the dark head butts the air wildly, hair shaking this way and that, like at a rock concert. She is carried off to a side room.

Rodney says tentatively, "That isn't...?"

"No no," says Rosalind. "I thought it was too, for a moment, but her hair's short now." Then she says, "I almost wish it was her. At least she'd be showing some kind of life."

Rodney knows exactly what she means. Most of the patients they have passed so far are so terribly devoid of life. Not what he expected at all. They shuffle past – silent, suspicious, stagnant.

Then Rodney sees his daughter for the first time since she was a baby. She is between crisp sheets with clean hair and bedclothes. In this state, at least, she bears little or no resemblance to Louise. It's the eyes. Rosalind did prepare him for the eyes, mercifully. Louise's eyes were healthy and glossy – you could see thoughts and emotions flashing across them like changes in the weather - unlike this sunken damson-ringed pair.

He watches Rosalind, now at home with this routine, as she takes a chair to Amanda's bedside. She is almost whispering to Amanda, telling her secrets. He hears her say, I've brought Rodney to see you. I promised you I would. He sees Rosalind as confident and assured, a woman no longer troubled by the quietly deriding or confused faces behind her. Now she is turning round to a girl who wheels a trolley along with ferocious eagerness. The girl is handing out orange juice in plastic cups to anyone and everyone.

"Hello Emma," says Rosalind. "This is Rodney "

"How do you do, Rodney," says Emma, shaking his

hand too long and too tight. "Can I interest you in some orange juice? I'm on drinks duty this afternoon."

"In that case we'll have three...that's most kind."

Rodney sits down on the bed. He takes his daughter's hand and gives it a slight squeeze. He thinks he feels a small reply from her fingers, a very slight stirring and there's a faint flicker of something in her eyes, that something known as recognition, a revival from the brink. He then takes one of the orange juices, places it in her hands and guides it to her lips. "Here you are, Amanda," he says. "Try that for starters."

Emma looks on goggle-eyed. "Drink up, Amanda! Oh bravo, Amanda! Bravo!"

####

About the author:

Kate Rigby was born in Crosby, Liverpool and now lives in Devon. She studied Psychology at Southampton, though she's given up paid work on health grounds. She's written 14 books (several published) and some short stories published or shortlisted. She's been writing novels for over thirty years now. She loves cats, singing, music, photography and LFC.

Further details about Kate's work can be found at her website:

http://kjrbooks.yolasite.com/

Her occasional blogs can be found at:

http://bubbitybooks.blogspot.com/

Printed in Great Britain
by Amazon